D0684331

THE DRAGON IN THE SOCK DRAWER

KATE KLIMO

with illustrations
by
JOHN SHROADES

SCHOLASTIC INC.
New York Toronto London Auckland
Sydney Mexico City New Delhi Hong Kong

ISBN 978-0-545-28989-4

Text copyright © 2008 by Kate Klimo.
Illustrations copyright © 2008 by John Shroades.
All rights reserved. Published by Scholastic Inc., 557 Broadway, New York, NY 10012,
by arrangement with Yearling, an imprint of Random House Children's Books,
a division of Random House, Inc. SCHOLASTIC and associated logos
are trademarks and/or registered trademarks of Scholastic Inc.

12 11 10 9 8 7 6 5 4 3 2 1   10 11 12 13 14 15/0

Printed in the U.S.A.   40

First Scholastic printing, October 2010

For Sandy and Jake's grandkids and great-grandkids.
And for Jesse and Daisy Robinson.

CONTENTS

THE WORLD
IS TALKING TO US.
EVERYTHING IN IT
HAS A STORY TO TELL.
ALL WE HAVE TO DO
IS SIT QUIETLY
AND LISTEN.
THIS STORY BEGINS
WITH A ROCK. . . .

CHAPTER ONE

THUNDER EGG

On the first day of summer, Jesse, his cousin Daisy, and his uncle Joe went to High Peak. Uncle Joe had come to look for rocks. Jesse and Daisy had mostly come for the ride. Upon reaching the windy summit of High Peak, Jesse took one look at the view and bent over to pick up a rock. It made him feel dizzy to look down from the mountain, which was doing a pretty good job of living up to its name.

Besides, maybe the rock would actually weigh him down enough to keep him from blowing away.

From Goldmine City (a big name for a small town), High Peak was sometimes visible. It rose in the distance like a delicious dessert topped with whipped cream. The whipped cream was snow, which was always there, even on the hottest day of the year.

Jesse was on the mountain for the first time. Up close, the snow didn't look so good. It looked sort of crusty and dirty, and it was much colder on the mountaintop than it was down in Goldmine City. Jesse's sweatshirt was not doing much to keep him warm.

Jesse had been living in Goldmine City with Daisy, Uncle Joe, and Aunt Maggie since Easter vacation in March. His parents were in Africa, setting up a children's clinic in a village in Tanzania. Jesse had traveled with his parents his whole life, but on his tenth birthday he decided that he wanted to live in America. He wanted to eat American food, go to an American school, and have adventures with Daisy, his favorite cousin, who he had been visiting for three weeks every summer of every year of his life.

These days, Jesse wore two watches on his left

wrist, one with a blue band and one with a black band. The watch with the black band told him the time in Goldmine City. The watch with the blue band told him the time in Tanzania. It was two o'clock here and midnight there. He imagined his parents asleep beneath mosquito netting in their hut, surrounded by snakes as long as cars and bugs as big as chipmunks. On the whole, even given the extreme elevation, he was happier here with Daisy.

Jesse went over to where Daisy was sitting to find out what she was doing. Anyone seeing them together would think they were friends rather than family, because they looked nothing alike. They were both ten years old, but Jesse was small for his age and sturdy, with brown eyes and shaggy brown hair. Daisy was fair-haired and tall and thin. The wind whipped her hair, which was as pale and fine as corn silk. The tips of her ears, which poked through her hair like an elf's, were bright pink. The tip of her nose matched.

Daisy looked up and smiled at Jesse through lips blue with cold. Then she went back to sketching a flower that was poking out of the snow. Her pencil was sticking out of the sleeve of her sweatshirt, which she had pulled over her hand to keep it warm. A wildflower handbook was open, its pages weighted down at the edges with small stones. Her eyes went from flower to sketch to handbook and back again. What rocks were for her father, flowers were for Daisy. She liked to say: "Not knowing the names of the flowers is like not knowing the names of your own brothers and sisters."

"What kind is it?" Jesse asked.

"I'm pretty sure it's *Prunella vulgaris*," she said. "It's totally magical. Its folk name is self-heal."

"Cool," he said. "What does it heal?"

"The Indians used to put it on boils," she said.

"Boils. Gross," he said.

Daisy carefully picked the wildflower and laid it between the pages of her notebook, right next to her sketch. She printed the name in neat block letters beneath the sketch and then turned the page. At home, she would transfer the specimen to her wildflower press, and, when it was dried, she would frame it. She had over twenty varieties of wildflowers already framed, her contribution to their Museum of Magic.

The two cousins' way of keeping in touch over the years had been by reading the same books of fantasy. They were convinced that sooner or later they would have a magical adventure of their own.

While they waited, they saw magic in everything around them: in flowers and seashells, in birds and animals, even in old bottles and doorknobs.

Daisy gave Jesse a sidelong look. "You okay?" she asked. She knew about his fear of heights. On the hike up the mountain, she had stopped practically every tenth step to ask him the same question.

Jesse nodded and held up the rock to show her that he was keeping busy, but Daisy had already moved on to the next wildflower. Jesse closed his eyes and thought about the e-mail message he would write to his parents when he got back to the house:

> Dear Mom and Dad, I finally got to High Peak.
> It is pretty high for an old volcano. But it is
> frozen stiff now. The snow looks sort of like
> whipped cream—

Jesse stopped cold.

"Let me out!"

Jesse's eyes snapped open. The voice sounded close and far away at the same time, like the music leaking out of somebody else's earphones.

Jesse looked around. Daisy and Uncle Joe were the only other people on the mountaintop. Uncle Joe was bending over, tapping a boulder with a small pickax. Daisy was flipping back and forth through her handbook. Then Jesse saw a man standing not far away. The man was poking around with a stick, the tail of his long black coat trailing in the snow. He was a bit strange-looking, but he clearly wasn't calling to Jesse.

"Jesse!"

There it was again!

"Jesseeee! Let. Me. Out!"

Jesse looked down. Either he was going crazy or the voice was coming from the rock in his hand. He held it up to his ear.

"Let! Me! Out!" said the rock. Or was the voice coming from something *inside* the rock?

Jesse held the rock at arm's length and stared at it. Uncle Joe liked to say: "If you see a rock that talks to you, pick it up and bring it home." Jesse had always been pretty sure that Uncle Joe did not mean this for real. But now he wondered.

The rock looked ordinary. It was round and nubby, the color of oatmeal with blackberry bits in it, including the green leafy part. It was warm from the sun and fit his hand like a softball.

"Jesse. Tiger!" said the rock.

"Huh? What did you say?" he whispered to the rock. Almost no one knew that Jesse's middle name was Tiger.

"Jesse! Tiger!!" said the rock again, vibrating in Jesse's hand.

"Daze?" he called out to his cousin, holding the rock up over his head. "This rock—" He stopped. He didn't know quite how to put it. He didn't want her to think that his fear of heights had made him wacky or anything.

Then again, maybe that's exactly what's happening, he thought.

Daisy took one look at the rock, then leaped up and ran over to him. She did a dance, like a happy little prospector who had just struck gold. "Jesse!" she said. "You found one! A thunder egg!" She pounded him on the back.

Uncle Joe was always talking about thunder eggs. There were lots of them in the area. They were also called geodes, and they were filled with agate. When you cracked one open, there were beautiful crystals inside.

"Do thunder eggs talk?" Jesse asked, trying to make his question sound like a joke.

Daisy grinned at him and gave him a playful shove. "Sure they do. This one's saying, 'Take me home, Jesse. Take me home and open me up.' Come on. Let's show my pops."

She dragged Jesse over to Uncle Joe. "Poppy, look what Jesse just found."

When Uncle Joe saw Jesse's rock, he straightened up. Then he took off his cap and tugged his long, graying ponytail. His cap was purple, with the words ROCK STAR inscribed in orange letters on the bill. It was a pretty funny joke, if you were a geologist like Uncle Joe.

"Sure looks like a geode to me," said Uncle Joe. "Congratulations, Jesse. She's a beauty."

Jesse squinted up at his uncle. "How do you know it's a girl?"

"Because," said Uncle Joe with a wink, "I speak the secret language of rocks."

Then how come this rock is talking to me *instead of to you?* Jesse wanted to ask. But he didn't say anything. Instead, he wrapped the thunder egg in a clean blue bandanna and gently placed it in the pouch of his sweatshirt.

"Okay, guys!" said Uncle Joe. He put his cap back on. "I think we can call it a day here. Let's head back down and take Jesse's thunder egg to the Rock Shop."

As they made their way across the summit back to the hiking path, they passed the strange man in the black coat, who stopped poking with his stick and stared at them as they went by. The sunlight glinting off his round wire-rim glasses made him look eerily as if he didn't have any eyes. Jesse quickly looked away.

In the pouch of his sweatshirt, the thunder egg zapped him so hard he yelped.

Daisy turned and gave him a look. "Are you *sure* you're okay?"

"I'm fine!" he said, his face burning.

The Rock Shop was an old garden shed behind the house. It had a worktable, shelves for Uncle Joe's rocks, filing cabinets for his notes, and all the tools of his trade, including a special one for cutting open a thunder egg.

Uncle Joe had cut open thousands of thunder eggs in his life but he still got a kick out of doing it. He put on his goggles and heavy work gloves before picking up his big band saw.

Jesse wasn't convinced that cutting open the rock was the right thing to do. What if doing that hurt whatever was inside? He covered his mouth, pretending to stifle a yawn as he whispered to the thunder egg, "Are you okay with this?"

The thunder egg vibrated warmly in his hand. Jesse decided to take that as a yes.

Jesse was still hesitant to hand the rock over to his uncle. "You'll be careful, won't you?" Jesse said.

"I mean, this won't, um, hurt or damage the crystals inside, will it?"

Uncle Joe smiled kindly. "I won't harm a single one of them. I promise." He held out a gloved hand.

Daisy gave her cousin a gentle shove. "Come on, Jessie Tiger. Let's get a look at those crystals."

"Goggles first, guys," Uncle Joe said.

Daisy went to a shelf and got two pairs of goggles. She tossed a pair to Jesse. Jesse almost dropped them, because just then the rock hissed, *"Jesssss—Jesssss—Jesssss—Jesssss."*

Jesse's glance slid from Daisy to Uncle Joe. Neither one of them seemed to have heard the rock. Arm trembling, Jesse handed the thunder egg to Uncle Joe. He winced as his uncle set down the saw and placed the rock between the iron jaws of a vise. He winced again as Uncle Joe spun the bolt and tightened the jaws around the thunder egg.

"Stand back, guys," said Uncle Joe.

Jesse and Daisy took one step away from him.

Uncle Joe picked up the saw and turned on the motor. It roared to life, vibrating mightily. Then Uncle Joe put the whirring blade to the top of the rock.

"Wait!" Jesse hollered over the noise of the machine.

Uncle Joe looked up. He switched off the saw

and pushed up his goggles. "What is it, Jesse?" he asked.

Jesse faltered. "It seems like a pretty delicate thing," he said. "I really, really, *really* don't want to hurt it."

Daisy rolled her eyes. "Poppy's only cut open a million rocks. I think he knows what he's doing, Jesse. *Really.*"

Uncle Joe spoke very calmly. "How about this? How about if I use the machine to cut a shallow groove in the rock? Then I'll turn it off and we can crack it open the rest of the way, carefully and gently, with a small chisel and a soft mallet."

Jesse's chest heaved with relief. He nodded gratefully. "Thanks, Uncle Joe. That sounds good."

Uncle Joe smiled at Jesse. "Okay if I switch on the saw?"

"Sure," said Jesse. "Go ahead." But he regretted this decision as soon as he heard the rock scream again above the noise of the saw. Just as Jesse was about to lunge over to Uncle Joe, the saw coughed and made a crackling sound.

Uncle Joe switched it off. "Well, I'll be," he said, holding up the saw so Jesse and Daisy could see it. The blade had split in two. Jesse and Daisy stepped toward the worktable. The egg wasn't even nicked.

"That's okay," said Jesse. "I don't have to see the crystals."

"We just need a stronger blade with bigger teeth," Daisy said. "We're going to open this stubborn old thunder egg, won't we, my adorable poppy?"

Uncle Joe took out the old broken blade and fit in a new one with teeth the size of a very big dog's. Daisy pulled Jesse back to where they had been standing. Jesse wanted to rescue his rock, but he was afraid Daisy and Uncle Joe would think he was nuts.

Uncle Joe put the saw to the rock once again. The saw howled like a hound dog. Or was it the rock that was howling? Smoke poured out of the saw.

Uncle Joe turned it off again and waved away the smoke. "I hope I'm not burning out the motor," he said.

"I wouldn't want you to do that, Uncle Joe," Jesse said. "Thanks for trying." Now he felt as if the voice inside was being a poor guest. Did it or did it not want out? And if it did, why wasn't it cooperating? And why was it being so hard on Uncle Joe's equipment?

"Can we try just one more time, Poppy?" Daisy pleaded.

Uncle Joe sighed. Then he put in the biggest, sharpest, strongest blade he had. It had long, jagged teeth, like a hyena's.

Daisy pulled Jesse one more step back. Uncle Joe switched on the saw. This time, when the blade touched the rock, purple and green sparks flew every which way. The machine shrieked like a banshee. Then the blade exploded, sending bits of sharp metal flying as the rock shot out of the vise.

The cousins yelped and dived for cover.

The rock flew clear across the room and crashed through the window.

CHAPTER TWO

THE MILLION-DOLLAR CAR

For a few moments, they all just stared at the broken window.

Finally, Uncle Joe spoke. "You guys get out of here. I'll clean up the mess. I don't want you to get cut. Look out for broken glass on your way out." He stooped, picking up two jagged bits of saw blade. He tried to fit them together, like pieces of a puzzle. "I don't get it," he muttered to himself.

16

"Sorry, Jess," said Daisy. "Thunder eggs are so cool when you can see inside them. Almost as interesting as wildflowers. It would have been a great addition to the museum."

Jesse slowly walked outside and picked up the thunder egg. He sniffed it. It smelled funny, like red-hot chili peppers. It was piping hot, almost too hot to hold. He turned the thunder egg around in his hands. There wasn't a single mark on it. He cast a look over his shoulder. It seemed like Daisy was staying behind to help her father after all.

Jesse put his mouth to the rock and whispered, "Are you okay in there?"

He put the rock to his ear. It was silent.

Jesse wondered if the rock was in shock. Maybe after a good night's rest, the rock would feel better and talk to him again. Or maybe the rock was angry and needed some quiet time—a chance to cool down. *Maybe you imagined it all,* he told himself. But just in case he hadn't, he whispered "Sorry" to the rock.

Jesse plodded up the back steps of the house and opened the screen door to the mudroom, which was next to the kitchen. Sighing, he wiped his feet on the mat. Even though his shoes were probably perfectly clean, he knew that Aunt Maggie would appreciate it and he wanted to make her happy. After all, she was his mother's only sister.

Aunt Maggie was standing at the stove, and there were pots and pans on every burner. Jesse figured she must be leaving soon on a trip for work. She always cooked a big, fancy dinner the night before she left on a business trip. Whatever she was cooking smelled delicious, but Jesse wasn't hungry.

"How was High Peak?" she asked. Then she saw his face. "Are you okay, honey?"

"I'm fine," he said, but he felt a heavy weight pressing down on his chest.

Jesse went through the kitchen and down the hall toward the front of the house. In the living room, the TV was tuned to the news, even though no one was there to watch it. He switched it off. Across the hall, in the dining room, the table was set for dinner. He trudged up the stairs and paused in the doorway of his bedroom. The back door slammed. He heard Aunt Maggie and Daisy talking down in the kitchen. He couldn't make out the words, but he could tell from their tone that they were talking about him.

Jesse went to his bedroom and closed the door. The room he slept in belonged to Daisy's two big brothers, Aaron and Noah. Aaron was already married, with a baby of his own. Noah was in college in Scotland and hardly ever came home. Even so, Jesse kept to Aaron's side of the room. He slept in Aaron's old bed, with Aaron's initials carved into the headboard. He used Aaron's old bureau, with the yellowed *Star Wars* shelf paper lining the drawers.

Jesse took the rock out of the pouch of his sweatshirt. He held it to his ear again. The rock was cold and silent. He sniffed it. It still smelled faintly of chili peppers. He opened the top drawer of the bureau and laid it among his many socks. For some reason, his grandmother sent him socks in the mail every two weeks. She sent regular shipments of socks to all her grandchildren, Daisy included. "Children never have enough socks," she liked to say.

Jesse closed the drawer and sighed. Then he left the room. At the top of the stairs, he turned around. He went back to the bedroom and opened the sock drawer a crack, just in case the rock needed to breathe.

"I found some really interesting basalt specimens for this new project I'm working on," Uncle Joe was saying as he chewed on a chicken drumstick.

Aunt Maggie laughed. "Just what this house needs," she said. "More rocks!"

The house was full of rocks, a fact that did not exactly thrill Aunt Maggie. She was in the "ad biz." She understood advertising. She did not understand the secret language of rocks. But she loved her husband, so she put up with him, rocks and all.

"Eat up, kids," Aunt Maggie said. "This is your last chance for real food this week. I'm off to Paris tomorrow for an ad shoot."

Jesse had guessed right. Aunt Maggie was going on a business trip. That was okay, because Uncle Joe was a stay-at-home parent, at least mostly. He worked part-time during the school year, teaching earth science at the College of Mining and Science in town.

"Sorry about your thunder egg," said Aunt Maggie.

"That thing is *not* a thunder egg," said Uncle Joe, wagging his fork at her.

"It isn't?" Jesse asked.

"Then what is it, Poppy?" said Daisy.

"I don't know," said Uncle Joe. "I need to do some tests to find out."

"*No!*" Jesse shouted.

Everyone turned and stared at him.

Jesse shrugged and smiled apologetically. "I'm sorry. It's just that I don't want my rock to have to go through any tests. . . ."

Uncle Joe laid a hand on Jesse's shoulder. "Hey, guy, it's your rock. I just thought you might be curious, is all."

Daisy's eyes narrowed, as if a secret theory of hers had just been confirmed. "You act like that rock's a living being," she said softly.

Jesse pushed green beans with almonds around on his plate. He gave her a look that said, *Let's discuss this later.*

Daisy nodded and smiled. "Jesse's got himself a pet rock!" she teased.

"The best kind of pet, if you ask me," said Aunt Maggie. She looked around at her family. "Rocks make the perfect pet, don't they? And we ought to know."

Everyone laughed, and Jesse was relieved when Aunt Maggie turned the talk to Paris. Jesse listened with one ear. He had the other ear cocked toward the stairs. If the thunder egg started calling to him, he would go running. But so far he hadn't heard a peep.

After everybody had pitched in to do the dishes, Daisy went to help her mom pack and Jesse returned to his bedroom to e-mail his parents. He always wanted his e-mail to be the very first thing they read in the morning before they went off to the clinic. But first he peeked into the sock drawer.

The thunder egg was gone!

Frantically, Jesse rummaged through the rolled-up socks. There it was! It had sunk to the very bottom of the drawer. He placed it back on top, tucked between a pair of tube socks with brown and yellow stripes and Daisy's purple ones, which Uncle Joe had absentmindedly tossed in the wrong sock drawer. "Don't move," Jesse told the rock firmly.

With that taken care of, he went to his computer and switched it on. His screen saver was a series of photographs of him and his parents in a Jeep on a game preserve near Nairobi. He began writing:

> Dear Mom and Dad, Uncle Joe took us with him to High Peak today. I found a thunder egg. It's supposed to have crystals inside, but mine was so hard it broke three of the blades on Uncle Joe's band saw and I didn't get to see the crystals, but that's okay. . . .

He skipped the part about the rock talking and went on to tell his parents how cold it was up there on the mountain and how the view took his breath away. He also didn't mention how scared he had been. Or the wave of homesickness that seemed to be swamping him tonight. More than once he stopped keying and checked the sock drawer to see if the thunder egg had moved from its spot. Jesse was disappointed to find that it hadn't moved at all.

After he had logged off, he wandered over to the window. His bedroom—along with Daisy's next door, linked to his by a shared bathroom—was at the front of the house, with a view of the street. It was a quiet street that dead-ended in a vacant lot. Everyone on the road parked their cars in their driveways. It was strange to see any cars parked on the street. That's why he noticed the big black car right away. It was one of those cars his dad called million-dollar cars because people with a lot of money usually drove around in them. Someone was sitting in the driver's seat, with the headlights off and the motor running.

Jesse grabbed his pajamas and went into the bathroom to change in the dark. He didn't usually dress in the bathroom, but there usually wasn't a strange black car parked outside his window. After he finished brushing his teeth, he went back into the bedroom and turned out the light. He paused at the window. The car was still there.

Jesse's eyes were closed but he was awake when Daisy came in and planted herself on top of his feet. Jesse knew she was waiting for him to explain himself. He wasn't sure how to do this, so he just kept silent and breathed loudly and deeply.

Not at all fooled, she sighed and said, "We need to go to the Dell tomorrow." Daisy waited for Jesse to answer.

"Um, Daze?" he said, opening his eyes. The light from the hallway lit her long blond hair, turning it silver. "About this pet rock thing . . ."

"Yes . . . ?" she said.

Jesse felt her tense up, waiting for him to go on. "Well, it wasn't a joke. I think—at least I'm pretty sure it's for real—the rock talked to me."

Jesse heard Daisy suck in her breath. Was she angry with him? Was she worried? Was she thinking he had finally cracked from homesickness? Was she going to tell Aunt Maggie and Uncle Joe to send him back to his mother and father? He saw himself on line at airport security. He saw a man opening his luggage and finding the rock. Was he even allowed to take the rock out of the country?

Daisy let out her breath and said, "I know it, Jesse. I know the rock made a noise." She tucked her hair behind her elfin ears, then looked right at him and smiled. "I heard it, too," she said.

"*Really?*" Jesse sat up. His heart did a little jig.

"When the saw was screaming? It sounded like the rock was screaming too, only even louder. It was really weird," she said with a thrilled shiver.

Jesse was so happy, he wanted to jump out of bed and do the happy-prospector dance. But he calmed himself down and said, "I know what you mean. I've been thinking about it for hours—we think of magic flowers and magic amulets and magic cauldrons and magic wands . . ."

"But who ever heard of a magic rock? I mean, how can a *rock* make *noise*?" Daisy said.

Jesse nodded, excited. "Right. It doesn't have lips or a tongue or anything."

"On the other hand, the Native Americans believed that everything has a spirit," Daisy said. She was on her knees now, waving her arms around. "Mammals and fish and birds and even things without faces, like rocks and fire and trees. Holy moly, Jess, maybe the rock's spirit is crying out to you!!" She sank back down on the bed and added softly, "Maybe to me, too?"

"Oh, definitely to you, too!" said Jesse.

"You know, Poppy says it's not a thunder egg. But I disagree. I think it's just a very special thunder egg. One in a million, maybe." After a short silence, she added, "Did I tell you where the term 'thunder egg' comes from?"

"I don't think so," he said.

"From the ancient Native Americans. They believed that thunder eggs didn't come from the earth. They believed that thunder eggs rained down from the heavens," she said.

Jesse shivered, and Daisy reached out and took his hand.

"Do you think . . . ?" Jesse started to ask.

"Who knows?" Daisy sighed and squeezed his fingers. "Maybe it came to us from outer space. I was thinking . . ."

"What?" Jesse said.

"You know how we checked out all the closets?" she said.

Jesse nodded. Last week, they had finished reading *The Lion, the Witch and the Wardrobe* for the fourth time. Afterward, they had investigated every closet in the house, hoping one of them would be the wardrobe leading to Narnia, a gateway to another world. All they had gotten for their trouble was noses full of musty air, dust, and the overpowering odor of mothballs.

"Maybe what we needed to get through the doorway was a *key*," said Daisy.

"A key?" Jesse asked.

"Yeah, like a key to the magic world. Don't you see, Jesse? The thunder egg! Maybe it's a key!"

Jesse nodded. He didn't know how to tell her this, but he didn't think of the thunder egg as a key. It felt distinctly more like a *she*. But he didn't want to dampen her enthusiasm, so he said, "Who knows? Maybe it is!"

"We'll check it out tomorrow," Daisy went on. "Meanwhile, let's get some sleep. Mom's leaving early. Then we'll see if the key fits." She hopped off the bed and gave his knee a pat. "Plan?"

"Plan," said Jesse.

Jesse fell asleep and started dreaming right away. He dreamed he and Daisy were pushing the thunder egg in a stroller. They pushed it past the million-dollar car. A man with no eyes jumped out, snatched the thunder egg, and drove away. The thunder egg started crying and calling his name.

Jesse woke up drenched in sweat. He went to the window. The million-dollar car was gone. Why hadn't he thought to tell Daisy about it? Or, better yet, brought her over to the window and shown it to her while it was still there? With a sudden gasp, he ran to the sock drawer and yanked it open.

The thunder egg *was* still there, nestled in its place between the tube socks and Daisy's purple kneesocks. Just to be safe, he took the thunder egg back to bed with him. He fell asleep with it pressed warmly against his cheek.

CHAPTER THREE

THE BIG BANG

The next morning was beautiful, as fresh and crisp as clean laundry snapping on the line. It was a great day for going to the Dell.

Jesse got out of bed and went to the window. No million-dollar car. He laid the thunder egg back in the sock drawer, got dressed, washed his face, and strapped on his watches.

Downstairs, Aunt Maggie was kissing Uncle

Joe good-bye. Then she kissed Daisy. Jesse got to the bottom of the stairs just in time for his kiss.

"Take care of that thunder egg," Aunt Maggie said. She hugged him extra hard, twice. "One from me and one from your mom," she whispered in his ear.

"Safe trip, Aunt Maggie," he said.

She smiled and smoothed his shaggy hair.

Outside, a car horn honked.

Aunt Maggie looked around one last time. She liked leaving everything in apple-pie order. "Don't forget to change your socks," she told them. "Brush your hair when you get up, and eat at the table. No reading while you eat. No eating over the sink. Keep everything in apple-pie order."

"We will!" they all told her as they followed her out. "Have a great time. See you Friday!"

"And brush your teeth," Aunt Maggie added as she got into the airport cab.

They stood in the driveway and waved until the cab was out of sight.

Then Jesse, Daisy, and Uncle Joe turned around, went back inside, and ate their cereal standing over the sink. It's not that they hadn't heard Aunt Maggie loud and clear. But how else, they all agreed, were they going to keep the house in apple-pie order?

After breakfast, Uncle Joe said he was headed for the Rock Shop. "So where are you two guys gallivanting off to today?" he asked.

"We're going to hang out here, then go to the Dell," Daisy told him.

"Well, have fun," he said. "I'll see you at dinnertime." It was normal for Uncle Joe to spend an entire summer day in the Rock Shop, especially when he had a new project to work on.

The moment Uncle Joe was out the back door, Daisy said, "Get the thunder egg. Where do you want to start?"

Jesse gave her a puzzled look. Then last night's business about the key to the magic doorway came back to him. "I guess the closet in my room?"

She nodded. "Good plan."

Daisy followed Jesse into his room. He took the thunder egg out of the sock drawer. Daisy solemnly marched over to the closet and pulled open the door with a flourish.

Jesse knew just what to do. With one hand, he shoved aside the thicket of hockey sticks and lacrosse sticks and baseball bats, clearing a path to the wall at the back of the closet. "Should I close my eyes?" he asked Daisy.

"I would," she said.

Jesse closed his eyes, held the thunder egg in

front of him, and took baby steps into the closet. He did his best to imagine the back wall melting away into trees and the clutter on the floor turning to pine needles and dirt, just as the wardrobe had dissolved for Lucy. *Bump!* The thunder egg hit the back of the closet. He lowered the rock slowly. "Uh—I don't think it's working."

"Are you sure you're *believing* hard enough?" she asked over his shoulder.

"Very, very hard," Jesse said to the wall.

Daisy backed out of the closet, hauling Jesse after her, and spun him around to face her. "What went wrong?" she asked.

He looked down at the thunder egg. It remained stonily silent. Jesse knew just how it felt. "I'm not sure . . . ," he said.

Daisy knitted her brow. "Well, please try a little harder next time."

After that, Jesse and Daisy walked into every closet in the house, with the same results. They saved Aunt Maggie's vast walk-in closet for last.

"Let *me* try this time," said Daisy. She took the thunder egg from Jesse and went into the closet. When she reached the back of it, she gave the wall an impatient kick with her sneaker. Then she sighed. "Okay, so it's not a key," she said. "It's just a talking rock." She spun around and put the thunder egg back into Jesse's hand. "And I'm sorry I'm so grumpy. It's just so darned *disappointing*! It's enough to make me cry."

Jesse went to his bedroom and opened his sock drawer. "Sorry to put you through all that," he said to the thunder egg, placing it back in the drawer. The rock still didn't say anything. Jesse was beginning to wonder if it was ever going to speak again. But he was fond of it, all the same.

He went down to the kitchen and found Daisy already at work preparing their picnic lunch for the Dell. She was making fresh lemonade. Her expression was fierce as she bore down on the electric juicer. Jesse whistled softly as he grabbed a can of tuna fish, opened it, and got some mayonnaise from the refrigerator. He kept whistling as he mixed the tuna salad and spread it on the bread. He slapped the tops on the sandwiches, sliced each in half, and wrapped them in waxed paper. Whistling still, he packed them, along with two hard-boiled eggs, in their single backpack, which they shared, taking turns carrying it wherever they went.

"*Quiet!*" Daisy snapped at him.

He was about to say, *Gee, can't a person even whistle*—but then he heard it, too.

It was a rattling sound—a very faint but very

distinct rattling sound. Jesse and Daisy stared at each other, mouths open. Jesse's eyes went to the ceiling. The sound was growing louder. It was coming from upstairs.

The cousins headed for the stairs. By the time they reached the foot of the staircase, the rattling had turned into a rumbling. It shook the family photographs on the wall. From where they were standing, Jesse could tell that the noise was coming from the front of the house. In fact, it was coming from his bedroom.

They started up the stairs, gripping the vibrating railing. The sound was thunderous now.

At the top of the stairs, they turned to see that the doorknob of Jesse's room was jiggling. That's when the look on Daisy's face switched from excitement to fear.

Jesse bravely crept over and put his hand on the doorknob, but he pulled it back. "It's hot!" he shouted over the din, rubbing his fingers on the seat of his pants. Now he was scared, too. If the house blew up, it would be his fault. Talk about getting things out of apple-pie order! Aunt Maggie would send him packing, for sure.

"This is ridiculous," said Daisy, squaring her shoulders. Then she went to the laundry cupboard and took out a washcloth. She wrapped it around the doorknob and turned it. The knob clicked, then—

KABLAM-WHOOSH!!!

The bedroom door blew outward, knocking both cousins onto their backsides. The air was filled with green-and-gold dust and the powerful smell of hot chili peppers.

Jesse and Daisy scrambled to their feet and ran into the room, coughing and waving away the dust. The sock drawer was on the floor. Socks were everywhere, and pieces of beautiful green and gold crystals sparkled among them.

In the middle of everything, something that looked like a lizard was standing on its hind legs and peering around. It was no bigger than a newborn kitten. Its bottom half was stout and covered with shiny scales. They were green (or blue, depending on how you moved your head), with the rainbow sheen of oil on a puddle. Sprouting from its shoulder blades were two dark green bumps, not so much wings as the *idea* of wings. Two long dark green ridges ran down its back and along its pointed tail. Its head looked like a sea horse's, only broader.

Jesse knew very well what he was looking at. But he didn't want to say it. So instead, he said, "Whoa!"

"Holy moly!" Daisy laughed uneasily. She added, "It's a good thing my mom just left." Then she pointed to the creature and said, "Oh, look! Poor thing!"

The lizard had gotten tangled up in one of Daisy's purple kneesocks and was wiggling and shaking to try to free itself.

"Shouldn't we help it?" Daisy asked.

Jesse had the same urge. But he realized that even though it was a tiny thing, he was a little afraid of it. "It's beautiful!" said Jesse. He wasn't sure that was the right word.

"Yes, it is," Daisy said softly. "So beautiful."

You know when you're in a pet shop and some animal, usually of the warm and fuzzy variety, looks at you and you just know you could be friends for life? That's the way Jesse felt when he looked at the creature. Only *Jesse* was the one who was warm and fuzzy—and the lizard creature was the one doing the shopping!

When the lizard finally shook itself free of the sock, it flung out its forepaws and said, "Jesse!"

It was the same voice he had heard yesterday, but much clearer. Jesse thought that if gold could talk, it would sound like this voice: fresh and clear and rich and metallic.

"Jesse!" it cried again. Then it cocked its green

head and set its bright eyes on Daisy. "Who?" it wanted to know.

"Her?" asked Jesse, pointing to his cousin. "That's Daisy."

"Day. Zee," it said, as if her name had two very distinct parts.

Daisy laughed. "That's right. You can talk!"

"Can. Talk," it said. Then it said, "Who. Am. I?"

"You," said Daisy, shooting a quick look at Jesse, "are a baby dragon. Right, Jess?"

Jesse nodded, grinning, happy that she had put his thoughts into words. "Right!"

"*Who*. Am. I?" the baby dragon repeated, each word coming out like a gold coin dropping into a cup. It kept looking from one cousin to the other, cocking its head, first to one side, then to the other. A green horn poked out between its eyes. A pulse throbbed in its pale green throat, and its underbelly gave off a glow like sunlight shining through spring leaves. Its tail switched back and forth impatiently.

"I think she wants us to give her a name," said Jesse.

"How do you know it's a girl?" asked Daisy.

"Because Uncle Joe said it was and he speaks the secret language of rocks, and, I don't know . . . it *looks* like a girl, doesn't it?" he said.

"Sort of . . . I guess, now that you mention it.

So what are we going to name her?" Daisy asked.

After some thought, Jesse said, "Let's call her Emerald."

"Emerald!" said Daisy. "I like that!"

"Like. That," said the baby dragon. "Em. Ma. World."

The cousins laughed giddily. She was so cute, and eerie at the same time.

"How about Emmy for short?" said Jesse.

"Good idea," said Daisy. "Because she's kind of short."

The cousins laughed again.

"Jess. Eee. Day. Zee. Em. Meeeeeee!" the little dragon sang, bouncing up and down on her sturdy hind legs.

The cousins grinned happily.

"This is even better than a key!" said Daisy.

Jesse nodded. "*Way* better!"

"Where did you come from?" Daisy asked. "I mean . . . besides the thunder egg?"

The dragon looked at her and said, "From. The. Time. Be. Fore."

Jesse felt a ripple of excitement run up his spine. "From the time before? The time before *what*?" he asked.

Emmy looked around, the pulse throbbing in her pale throat. "I. For. Get," she said. Then she repeated, "From. The. Time. Be. Fore. I. For. Get. When."

"When's the time before, do you think?" Jesse asked Daisy.

Daisy was flapping her hands, which she did only when she was very excited. "Maybe it isn't a magic *land* we've come upon. Maybe it's a magic *time,*" she said.

"Cool!" said Jesse.

"Em. Meee. Eat. NOW!" said the dragon.

The cousins came back to earth with a thud.

"Emmyeatemmyeatemmyeat NOW!" She was bouncing up and down like a small rubber toy. "Up! Up!! UP!!!"

"I think she wants you to pick her up," said Daisy to Jesse.

"No kidding. How do you hold a baby dragon?" Jesse asked as he moved toward Emmy to do her bidding.

Daisy thought for a minute. "My guess is, very carefully," she said.

"Ha-ha. Very funny," said Jesse as he leaned down and held out his cupped hands. The dragon scrambled into them, her claws digging into him.

"Ouch!" he said. She felt like a ball of needles in his hands. He dumped Emmy back onto the carpet.

"Up!" Emmy said. "Em. Meee. Up!"

Daisy looked around. "Try this," she said. She took her purple kneesock and put it over Jesse's hand.

Jesse picked up Emmy again. "Brilliant," he said to Daisy.

Jesse started walking with tiny steps, holding the dragon stiffly in front of him. Daisy ran ahead, but not before shutting the door on the mess in Jesse's room. "We'll clean up later," she said.

In the kitchen, Jesse sat down slowly and set Emmy carefully on the kitchen table. He propped his chin on the table so he could meet the little dragon eye to eye. "May we take your order?" he asked her.

"Fooooood," Emmy cooed, blinking her big eyes at him.

"That's a huge help," said Daisy. She paced up and down. "What *kind* of food, is the question."

Jesse screwed up his face and said, "Let's try and remember, from books and movies and all, what it is that dragons eat."

"Foood?" cooed Emmy hopefully. "For. Em. Meeee."

The cousins put their minds to it. Finally, Jesse said, "I'm seeing a big pile of bones, picked clean, lying outside of this big dark cave."

Daisy made a face. "Try seeing something else."

The cousins fell silent, thinking.

At length, Daisy said, "What about small wood-land creatures?"

Jesse said, "Remember my African rock python I wrote you about? I used to have to catch live rats to feed him. Not fun. Plus that snake had the worst breath—dead-rat breath."

"Forget that," said Daisy. "If she wants to eat rats, she'll have to catch them herself . . . *and* get some mouthwash."

"Jesse! Day. Zee! Food! Food! Food!!" wailed Emmy, her volume increasing.

"I think my brother and his wife left a box of baby Paul's rice mush," Daisy said, raising her voice over Emmy's racket. (Paul was Cousin Aaron's baby boy.)

"Let's try baby Paul's rice mush, then," said Jesse. "I'll make sure Emmy doesn't fall off the table. You mix the mush."

"Mush! Mush! Mush!" Emmy chanted, jumping up and down.

Jesse made a blockade on the table. It might have been safer to set Emmy down on the floor, but he was afraid she would scramble away or that they would accidentally step on her.

Daisy banged open cupboards until she found

the box of her nephew's rice cereal. She poured some into a bowl, added milk, shoved the bowl into the microwave, and jabbed at the buttons. While the microwave hummed, she dug around in a drawer for a baby spoon.

"Don't make it too hot," Jesse said.

Daisy yanked open the microwave door, took out the bowl, grabbed the spoon, and held them out to Jesse.

Jesse stared at them. "I guess this is my job," he said.

"The first thing she said was *your* name," she reminded him.

Emmy stopped jumping and peered curiously at the bowl of mush.

"Oh boy. This ought to be fun." Jesse yanked off the purple kneesock and took the bowl and spoon. Then he set the bowl on the table and scooped up some rice cereal. Hand shaking, he held out the spoon. "Okay, Emmy, come and get it."

"Mush! Mush! Mush!" Emmy made a running start and jumped into the bowl—SPLAT!—sending rice cereal flying everywhere.

Daisy grabbed a roll of paper towels and wiped the rice cereal off of Jesse's shirt and face. Jesse lifted Emmy out of the bowl and held her with one hand while Daisy wiped off her talons. Then he set

Emmy down again and held out the spoonful of rice. "Mush is for eating. Not swimming."

Emmy opened her mouth. The inside was bright pink, and her tongue was long and forked. Her mouth was the only part of her that wasn't some shade of green. There were two buds in front, but not much else in the way of teeth. Jesse tipped the spoon into her pink maw. Emmy closed her jaws. Jesse waited for her to swallow the cereal. He had the next spoonful all ready to go.

"Ptoooooie!" Emmy spat the rice cereal right in Jesse's face. "Bad!" she bawled. "Bad! Bad!! Bad!!! Not! Food!"

Daisy marched to the refrigerator and flung open the door while Jesse wiped his face. She tapped her foot. "Let's see what else we have." She pulled out leftover rice and beans. "She probably won't eat anything that's bad for her. We're just going to have to keep trying until we find something that works."

Jesse offered the rice and beans to Emmy.

"Blaaaaat!"

Jesse picked beans and rice grains off his face.

Then they tried some cranberry sauce.

"Guuuuuunk!"

Jesse fished a cranberry out of his ear.

"Marshmallow fluff?" Daisy proposed.

"Plooooook!"

Bits of marshmallow flew into Jesse's eyebrows and hair.

"No more sticky stuff, okay?" Jesse said.

Pickles.

Emmy spat pickle bits everywhere.

Mayonnaise.

"Hold the mayo!" Jesse shouted one second too late.

Emmy spewed chunks of salami, bologna, and tuna fish.

"You know what?" Jesse shouted over Emmy's hungry howls. "I'm thinking we need to buy some lizard kibble!"

"What's lizard kibble?" Daisy shouted back. She had lined up ketchup, peanut butter, relish, and chutney. She spun off lids and scooped up spoonfuls for Jesse to feed Emmy.

"Mealworms or live crickets!" Jesse shouted. He raised his arm and cowered as a storm of ketchup, peanut butter, relish, and chutney pelted him. It was like the world's biggest food fight, only it was completely one-sided and *very* unfair.

"What makes you think she'll like worms and crickets better than this stuff?" Daisy said, tossing Jesse a dish towel.

Jesse threw the towel over his head and wiped

his face and hair. Then he swabbed off the table, the chair, and the floor. "She's got to eat *something*. She'll starve. Look at her!" he said.

The little dragon lay in a mess of food. She was panting.

"Maybe we should go online and find out what to feed her," said Daisy.

Jesse sighed. "I guess it's worth a try."

"We have to clean up first. You clean in here and keep an eye on her. I'll vacuum upstairs. Plan?" said Daisy.

"Plan," said Jesse.

CHAPTER FOUR

THE CARE AND FEEDING
OF A DRAGON

Jesse took Emmy to the sink and washed her off. She splashed about in the water and held out her long pink tongue to catch the droplets.

"You're thirsty!" Jesse said. He dried her off, then poured her a bowl of water. "Water," Jesse said, setting both bowl and dragon in the center of the table. "Drink."

"Wa. Ter. Gooooood," Emmy said, and began to lap it up. She lifted her head up and let the water dribble down her throat. Then she set to lapping again.

"Drink up," Jesse told her, "and *don't move* from this spot."

"Em. Meee. Drink," she gurgled.

Keeping one eye on her, Jesse put everything back in the refrigerator and tackled the mess in the room. The kitchen was almost back in apple-pie order when he noticed a rather large splat of relish on the ceiling.

He sighed, then climbed onto the kitchen counter and went at it. When the spot was finally gone, he climbed down and leaned against the counter. He couldn't remember when he had worked so hard. And they still had a hungry baby dragon to feed! Jesse looked around. The bowl of water was empty, but Emmy was nowhere in sight.

Jesse heard Daisy switch off the vacuum cleaner upstairs. "Daze!" he called out. "Is Emmy up there with you?"

Daisy came pounding down the stairs and tore down the hall. "What do you mean? Where is she? Where did she go?"

"Look!" Jesse pointed to wet claw prints on the clean floor.

The cousins followed the tracks down the hall and into the living room, where the aroma of hot chili peppers told them they were getting warmer. They heard a faint crunching sound coming from the wall of bookshelves. In front of the books, the shelves were packed with boxes of rocks, all carefully labeled.

Emmy was crouching in a box marked LIMESTONE, munching away at a small rock. "Mmmmm. Gooooood," she said when she saw them. Her voice had gone all gruff and gravelly.

"Uh-oh," said Daisy.

Jesse regarded Emmy glumly. "Well, that's just dandy!" he said. Now he had something new to worry about. How could eating a rock be good for a baby *anything*? Even if rocks were good for baby dragons, she didn't have any teeth to grind them up with. She might choke! And even if she didn't choke to death, what was Uncle Joe going to say about the missing limestone?

Daisy said, "Emmy, that's Poppy's limestone rock specimen."

"Em. Meee. Like. Rrrockkk!" she said. The word "rock" seemed to be packing a few extra *r*'s and *k*'s.

Daisy shrugged. "At least there's plenty more where that came from. And I can't say my mom is going to mind the slight reduction in the rock population around here."

Emmy swallowed, smacked her lips, and burped. A puff of stone dust floated out of her mouth like a smoke ring.

With the baby dragon's hunger pangs quelled for the time being, Jesse and Daisy parked her in the sock drawer and went online to see what they could discover about the care and feeding of their dragon.

"Google 'dragons,'" said Daisy.

"Googledragonsgoogledragonsgoogle," Emmy babbled from the sock drawer.

"That's what we're doing, Em," Jesse assured her.

Then he groaned. Googling "dragons" got him 36,100,000 hits. He scrolled through the first few screens. Half of the listings seemed to be about the game *Dungeons and Dragons*. Other sites had to do with dragon legends, art, tattoos, and movies.

"Not helpful," Jesse said, frowning at the screen. "We need to narrow this down."

"Try 'dragon *food*,'" said Daisy.

"Foooooood," Emmy crooned from the sock drawer.

That entry produced at least three million

listings, many for something called Bearded Dragon Medley.

"What's a bearded dragon?" Daisy wanted to know.

Jesse, who had owned many exotic pets in the far-off lands where he had lived, said, "A lizard native to Australia. But I don't see anything here about feeding a *real live* dragon."

"I know!" said Daisy, leaning over the back of his chair. "Try Googling 'The Time Before'!"

Jesse did just that and counted 1,480,000,000 responses that started with "the big bang" and went on to *The Land Before Time*. "It would take us five years to go through all these, and by then there would be a million more," he said.

Daisy sighed. "We'd better go to the library."

Jesse pointed to the sock drawer. "And are we taking *her*?"

"You bet we are . . . unless, of course, you came across any listings for *dragon-sitters*?" Daisy said with a sly smile.

"I guess I could carry her in the pouch of my sweatshirt, like I did when she was inside the thunder egg," Jesse said. He switched off the computer and pulled on his hooded sweatshirt, thinking that it was a good thing early summers were cool.

"Come on, Emmy," he said, putting Daisy's purple kneesock over his hand and reaching into the sock drawer.

"Where. Go?" said Emmy, scrabbling on board.

"We're taking a little trip," he told her.

"Lit. Tell. Trip. Where?" she wanted to know, her eyes swiveling as if in search of the "lit tell trip."

"To find out some stuff we need to know," he told her.

"Find. Some. Stuff?" she asked, her eyes still searching.

"Yeah . . . about how to take care of you," he said.

Her eyes came to rest on him. "Jess. Eee. Tie. Ger. Gooooood. Dra. Gon. Kee. Per."

Jesse Tiger, Dragon Keeper! He liked the sound of that. "Aw, thanks, Emmy. Well, your Dragon Keeper says you have to stay under cover when we go out."

"Why. For?" she asked.

"We need to hide you," Daisy said.

Emmy said, "Hide. Em. Meee. From. Bad. Man."

"No. There's no bad man." Flashing on the man in the million-dollar car, Jesse wondered. "At least I don't *think* there is. But it's important that nobody sees you. So you have to ride in the pouch of my sweatshirt," he told her, putting her gently in one side. Emmy quickly crawled out the other side, scratching Jesse with her talons. "Ouch!"

"Em. Meee. Not. Like!" she said, scrambling into his hand.

"No kidding," he said.

"Maybe she'd like to ride in your hood instead," said Daisy. She got the other purple kneesock and pulled it over her hand. Then she took Emmy and held her so they were nose to nose.

"Hey there, Emmy!" Daisy said, smiling.

"Hey. There. Day. Zee," Emmy said.

"I'm going to put you in the hood of Jesse's sweatshirt," she explained. "You're going to be riding piggyback, and you have to try very hard not to scratch Jesse, okay?"

"Pig. Gee. Back. Oh. Kay. Day. Zee," she said.

Daisy put Emmy in Jesse's sweatshirt hood, which hung down his back. Jesse felt the slight weight of the dragon.

"Are you okay back there?" he asked her.

"Em. Me. Oh. Kay."

"Brilliant," said Jesse.

Daisy's house was only a short distance from downtown Goldmine City, where the library was. It was close enough to walk, but the cousins decided to ride bikes there. Daisy had her own bike, and Jesse rode Noah's old blue ten-gear Schwinn racer.

When he leaned over the handlebars to pedal, Jesse felt Emmy creep up his back and perch on his shoulder.

Jesse and Daisy had agreed that if anyone saw Emmy, they would explain that she was a green basilisk from Costa Rica. They figured this would work because (a) she was nothing if not green, and (b) who in Goldmine City, other than Jesse, had ever even seen a green basilisk? It seemed as good a story as any. They only hoped no one would hear her talking.

"Like. Bike! Like. Bike! Like!" Emmy said as they set out.

"Bikes are nifty," Jesse agreed.

"Bikes. Niff. Tee!" she said. "Go. Jesse. Go."

"She sure likes to yak," said Daisy. For Emmy's sake, they pedaled as slowly as they could while still keeping their bikes upright. Emmy talked a mile a minute. Out of the corner of his eye, Jesse saw her head darting left and right.

"Fair. Ee?" Emmy asked Jesse.

Jesse flicked a look over his shoulder and saw that she was staring at the plaster figurine on a lawn. He grinned. "That's not a fairy. That's a statue. It's a garden gnome," he told her.

A few seconds later, Emmy said "Cass. Sell?" as they wheeled past a big new shingled house with a turret.

"No," Jesse said. "That's not a castle. It's a house."

Just then a car turned the corner up ahead and came down the street. It was the first moving car they had seen. Jesse said, "Car. We use them to get places quickly."

Nostrils flaring, Emmy said, "Smell. Like. Dragon. Piddle."

The vehicle was practically on top of them when Jesse realized that it was the million-dollar car from the night before. He braked hard. "Hide!" he whispered to Emmy. She went as still as a stone against his back. Jesse froze, too, as the car glided past. Moving only his eyes, he tried to look through the tinted windows, but he couldn't see anything.

Daisy came circling back. "What's up?" she said, braking in front of him.

Jesse turned his head to stare at the car. Then he turned back to face Daisy and was preparing to tell her about it when their friend Miss Alodie called out to them from her garden on the corner up ahead. "Yoo-hoo! Cousins!"

"Hey, Miss Alodie!" Daisy waved at her.

Miss Alodie had the most beautiful garden in Goldmine City, the envy of everyone who saw it. Miss Alodie's daisies were bigger than sunflowers, her sunflowers were bigger than fruit trees, and her tea roses were as big as Frisbees. Practically everything Daisy knew about flowers, she had learned from Miss Alodie.

Jesse heard Emmy say, "Gar. Den. Gnome. Foooood?"

Miss Alodie was pruning a bush of giant yellow roses. She wore bright pink garden gloves, clunky sandals with socks, plaid pedal pushers, and a flower-patterned blouse. Her green beanie, which reminded Jesse of the top of a zucchini with the stem still attached, came up only to Jesse's chin. *She does look like a gnome!* he thought.

"Good day, my young friends!" Miss Alodie said. Her sparkling blue eyes were a perfect match for the paint on the shutters of her cottage.

"Beautiful roses, Miss Alodie!" said Daisy.

"Why, thank you, Miss Daisy. I like them, too," said Miss Alodie. "You know, roses are not native to the Americas. They originally came from the Far East."

"Interesting," said Jesse.

"Foooood?" Emmy asked.

Daisy said, "Jesse and I are making a Museum of Magic up at the barn. It's got a great section on wildflowers, and you're invited to visit."

"Just say the word and I'll be there with bells on," Miss Alodie said.

Jesse felt a prickling on the back of his neck as Emmy scrambled out of his hood and perched on his shoulder.

"Land's sakes!" Miss Alodie said. She came out from behind her rosebush, planted her feet wide, and tipped back her head to look at the baby dragon. "Is that what I think it is?"

Emmy stared down at Miss Alodie and blinked.

"She's a green basilisk from Costa Rica," Jesse said quickly. "We found her at the Dell."

"Is that a fact?" said Miss Alodie, her blue eyes dancing. "She's certainly a long way from home, isn't she? Well, take very good care of her. Keeping a pet is a responsibility. Do not take it lightly, my young friends."

"We won't," Jesse said. Then he gave Daisy a meaningful look and added, "We have to get going now, right, Daze?"

"Right," said Daisy. "We have some important research to do at the library. See you soon, Miss Alodie."

"I'll be seeing you two kids at the Museum of Magic!" Miss Alodie said, returning to her rosebush.

"Niff. Tee. Gnome!" said Emmy.

Uncle Joe liked to say that Goldmine City needed a new name because the gold mine had been boarded up for over a century and the town wasn't big enough to be called a village, much less a city. Jesse and Daisy rode down nearly empty Main Street and chained their bikes to the rack in front of the library. Like the few other buildings in town, the library had stone pillars and a grand flight of steps. It was a leftover from the days when the town had boomed.

Daisy drew Jesse behind a tree and said to Emmy, "There are no pets allowed in the library. So you need to get back in the hood and not show your face."

"Lie. Brare. Eee?" Emmy asked, cocking her head.

"It's where we keep books. Where we store lots of our knowledge," Jesse explained.

"And there's *no* yakking allowed in the library," said Daisy. "Because people want to read their books in peace and quiet."

"Read. Books? Scrip. Tor. Eeee. Um!" Emmy said, her head bobbing rapidly.

The cousins looked at each other and put Emmy's syllables together. *"Scriptorium!?!"* they chimed, then shrugged.

Daisy led the way up the steps. Just as she was opening one of the library's double doors, Jesse caught a glimpse of what looked like the million-dollar car reflected in the glass. He whipped around. It was just an ordinary dark green car. Jesse felt a little foolish. *Probably someone who lives on our street has just bought a big black car,* Jesse thought. *I am getting all worked up for nothing.*

Mr. Stenson, the weekday librarian, was seated behind his desk. He smiled when he saw the cousins come in. "How are my two most avid young readers?" he asked. "In this computer-crazy world, I can't tell you how nice it is to see a couple of kids who still prefer an old-fashioned book to a newfangled hard drive."

Jesse and Daisy exchanged a guilty look.

"What are you looking for today?" said Mr. Stenson. "We've got the first book in a brand-new fantasy trilogy. I think you're really going to like it."

"Is it about dragons?" Jesse wanted to know.

"We're looking for books about dragons," Daisy told him.

The librarian laughed and said, "You and every other kid in the world. Which one? We have lots of books about dragons."

"Oh, anything . . . dragonish, to be exact," said Daisy.

"Dragon stories, dragon legends, dragon operating instructions . . ." Jesse trailed off.

"You kids are in luck. Just the other day, I made up a list of the dragon books in our collection," said the librarian.

He opened a file folder and shuffled through some pages until he found what he was looking for. He gave it a quick look and smiled. "There are some great reads here," he said.

Emmy must have disagreed with the librarian, because she blew in Jesse's ear and whispered, "Dragon piddle!"

Jesse started coughing to hide his laughter, giving a little hop to shake Emmy down into his hood. "Thanks a lot, Mr. Stenson," he said.

Mr. Stenson's nose twitched. "Do you two smell something?" he asked.

The cousins looked at Mr. Stenson, their eyes wide.

"I don't smell anything. Do you, Daze?" said Jesse.

"Not me," said Daisy.

"Strange," said the librarian. "Not quite sure what it is." He lifted his nose in the air and sniffed some more. "Burritos? Tacos? Mexican salsa, maybe?"

"Sounds great to me!" said Jesse.

"Yeah," said Daisy. "When do we eat?"

Mr. Stenson grinned. "It's probably just my hungry tummy manufacturing appetizing aromas."

"This list looks great," said Jesse.

"Can we keep it?" said Daisy.

"Be my guest . . . and happy reading!"

After thanking him again, the cousins went to their regular table in the children's section. They huddled, running their eyes down the list. It filled an entire piece of paper.

"I've got a plan," said Daisy. She folded the sheet of paper in two and ripped it on the edge of the table. She handed Jesse the top half. "You hunt up those. I'll hunt up the rest. We'll pile the books here on the table and figure out which ones we want to check out first."

Luckily, the plan soon put Emmy to sleep. Whether it was from the peace and quiet of the library or his steady plodding through the stacks, Jesse didn't care. He was just grateful. When Jesse and Daisy had finished hunting and gathering, they had a small mountain of books on the table.

"Okay," said Daisy. "Let's set the ones that seem like they might give us useful facts on the right and the ones that are just made-up stuff on the left."

They went through the books with surprising speed. When they were finished, they had no books on the right and a big stack on the left. They were all probably perfectly wonderful books. It's just that, from what the cousins could tell, they didn't contain much in the way of practical advice on the care and feeding of a baby dragon.

"What about this one?" Jesse said, pointing to the last title on Daisy's half of the list. It wasn't in the pile.

"The Dragon Keeper's Guide?" she said. "Yeah, that's because it wasn't on the shelf. And the funny thing is," she added, "it was the only book that was actually listed as nonfiction."

They returned to Mr. Stenson's desk and asked him about the missing book. He looked it up on his computer and quickly confirmed that there was only one copy and that it was checked out and over-due. "The book's long out of print," he said.

The cousins went over to the computerized card catalog and looked up *The Dragon Keeper's Guide*. The author was listed as Professor L. B. An-dersson, D.D. (Doctor of Draconology). The book had been published in 1877!

"It's old," said Daisy. "What's in it?"

Jesse leaned toward the screen and read the small print aloud. "Hatchlings, younglings, hoarding, scrying, masking, flaming, soaring, spelling, dreaming, The Time Before."

There it was on the screen, in black and white. *The Time Before!*

After swiftly returning the books to the shelves, the cousins flew home and dashed upstairs to the computer. With Daisy standing behind his chair, Jesse Googled "Professor L. B. Andersson." Only *four* hits! The first three listings were about the book, which seemed to be the only one the man had ever written, or at least the only one Mr. Google knew anything about. Next to the fourth entry, a Web site was listed.

The site was called www.foundadragon.org. Jesse clicked on the link and the home page came up.

On the left side of the screen was a black-and-white drawing of a dragon. It looked very old. On the right was a photograph of a very stern-looking man with long white hair, a long white beard and mustache, and white eyebrows bristling over sparkling black eyes.

Jesse didn't know what to do, so he clicked on the old man's face and was startled when the photograph suddenly came to life. The dark eyes blazed, the long nose twitched, and the mouth beneath the mustache opened and began to speak. "So! You think you have found a dragon?" it boomed at them.

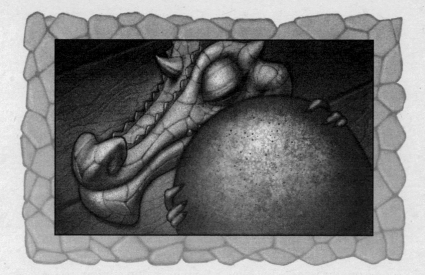

CHAPTER FIVE

THE SORCERER'S SPHERE

"Whoa!" Jesse rolled back in his chair and stared at the screen. "What am I supposed to do now?"

Daisy pointed to the blinking cursor at the bottom of the screen. "Try keying there," she said.

"Try keying *what*?" he asked. "Did you get a good look at this guy? He's scary!"

"Just tell him yes," Daisy said patiently, "and see what happens."

Jesse took a deep breath and rolled back to the computer. He flexed his fingers and keyed, in capital letters, "Y-E-S."

Once again, the photograph stirred to life and the lips moved. "Very good. What are its salient characteristics?"

"Um, what does 'salient' mean?" Jesse asked Daisy out of the corner of his mouth.

But it was the man on the screen who answered him: "By 'salient,' we mean 'most noticeable; prominent.'"

Jesse stiffened. "How did he do that? Can he actually hear what we're saying? I don't know if I like that," he added, turning from the screen and cupping his hands around his mouth.

"Of course he can't," said Daisy. "He probably just expects most people not to understand that word. So go ahead." She gave his shoulders a gentle squeeze.

"Go ahead and *what*? This guy is giving me the creeps." Then he caught himself and apologized to the screen. "Excuse me, mister. It's just that I'm not used to a talking . . . to a talking, um, Web, um . . . head."

The picture on the screen remained silent and still.

"Write in her salient characteristics, Jess," said Daisy. "Why not start with the little green horn?"

Jesse nodded and put his hands on the keys.

"Stop!" the voice roared. Jesse's fingers froze. In a softer tone, the professor said, "It is not necessary for you to type your responses. I can hear you."

"Yikes!" Daisy grabbed Jesse's neck. "He *can* hear us!"

"I can indeed," said the professor, "provided you take the trouble to make yourself understood, by which I mean that you must *enunciate*."

"What does *that* mean?" Jesse asked.

The professor replied, "It means that you must speak clearly and slowly and succinctly, *and not slur your words*! Simply click the mouse when you wish to speak."

Jesse gaped at the screen.

"Go ahead." Daisy nudged him. "It's like an interview."

Jesse clicked the mouse, cleared his throat, and said, loudly and clearly and slowly—exactly the way he spoke to their great-aunt Elizabeth, who was as deaf as a tree stump—"She has this little green horn on her head!"

The professor's face burst into a smile. "Very

good!" he said. "But there is no need to shout. I assure you, I am not deaf."

Jesse blushed.

"Do go on," said the professor.

Jesse nodded and clicked the mouse once again. At a more moderate volume, he said, "She hatched out of a geode. She has a forked tongue. She likes to eat limestone. She smells like hot chili peppers. She comes from The Time Before—"

"Don't forget to say she can talk," Daisy whispered.

"Oh, right!" said Jesse. "She talks!"

Just then the left side of the screen lit up. The picture of the dragon turned bright green on a field of dazzling red and began blinking, as if they had just hit the jackpot. The old man's eyebrows lifted, and he grinned. "Bravo!" he told them. "You have found yourself a dragon!"

Even though the cousins already knew this, it was nice to get proper credit for their discovery. When the screen stopped flashing, Jesse clicked the mouse and asked, "Could you tell us what to feed her? I mean, besides limestone."

"Ah!" said Professor Andersson, stroking his beard. "Most interesting! This is the first instance of actual limestone ingestion I have come across. I suspect that your dragon ate limestone because limestone contains calcium. Your dragon is a hatchling. Hatchlings need large doses of calcium to fuel their initial growth spurt. Feed her foods high in calcium, such as cheese, eggshells, broccoli, cauliflower, cabbage, kale, spinach, Brussels sprouts, and dark-leaf lettuce."

"Great!" said Daisy. "She can have my cabbage and Brussels sprouts any old day of the week!"

The cursor blinked. "What else should we ask?" Jesse wondered. Now that he was in the presence of an actual dragon expert, his mind was blank.

"Wait." Daisy squeezed her eyes shut to help her remember. "Ask him about some of the stuff in his book. Hoarding, masking, flaming. That kind of stuff."

Jesse turned to the screen and clicked the mouse again. "What is hoarding?" he asked.

The professor's bushy beard barely concealed a smile as he said, "First Kilimanjaro, then Everest, eh?"

"What's *that* supposed to mean?" Jesse asked.

Daisy thought for a second. "I think it means hold your horses," she said.

Professor Andersson said, "Let's take one thing at a time, shall we? For now, all that is necessary for you to know is that daily fresh air and exercise are necessary for the development of healthy bones.

Keeping a dragon is a considerable responsibility. Do not take it lightly."

Do not take it lightly.

The cousins turned and searched each other's faces. Where had they heard those words before? Suddenly the entire screen flashed red. The picture of the dragon and the old man vanished. Filling the space now, in large throbbing purple letters, were the words "BEWARE THE DRAGON SLAYER!!!!!"

Then the computer made an odd grinding noise and went blank. A dull message box appeared: "Computer cannot view this page at present. Check with your server or try again."

"Hey!" Jesse said, pounding the table. "What's the big idea?"

"Try to get back in," said Daisy.

Jesse rapidly keyed in www.foundadragon.org.

Maddeningly, the same message appeared.

"Where did he go?" Jesse wanted to know. "We need him to tell us about the Dragon Slayer! I mean, how can we protect Emmy if we don't know more?"

"We'll try again later," Daisy said. "I'm starved, aren't you? Let's go to the Dell and have our picnic. Emmy can have the shells of our hard-boiled eggs. Plan?"

"Plan," said Jesse. He logged off with a discouraged sigh, then they headed down to the kitchen to make lunch.

There was a dense patch of laurel bushes at the top of the rise that separated the backyard from the old cow pasture and barn they called the Dell. Jesse and Daisy had to drop to their knees and crawl through a tunnel in the laurels. Just when their knees started to scream, they arrived at the other end of the tunnel and stood up.

The Dell lay before them like a big bowl lined with clover and wildflowers, a rocky brook running through it like a crack. On one side there was the mountain. The Native Americans who had once lived in the area called it the Old Mother because, at certain times of the day, the side of the craggy mountain looked like the face of an old woman, with a waterfall running down it like tears. Behind the big red dairy barn lay the Deep Woods, so-called because they were too dense and dark for the cousins to venture into beyond a few steps. On top of the barn's patched roof was a weather vane of a horse going whichever way the wind blew him.

Emmy struggled out of Jesse's hood and perched on his shoulder. She looked here and there, her pale green throat throbbing like a frog's. She scrabbled her prickly way down Jesse's arm and jumped to the ground. She flung out her forepaws.

"Ma. Ma?" she cried, looking up at the mountain.

"Ma. Ma?" she cried, looking across the pasture to the Deep Woods.

"Ma. Ma?" she cried, looking down at the big red barn. Then she turned her eyes first on Jesse, then on Daisy, and bleated, "Em. Meee. Want. Ma. Ma!"

Jesse and Daisy looked at each other helplessly. What could they say? They had no idea where Emmy's mother was. One thing was fairly certain. Emmy's mother had been dead since The Time Before, whenever that was. But there was no way they could tell Emmy that, not when she was such a baby.

Emmy took off down the hill, making whooping sounds.

The cousins ran after her, but the little dragon kept the lead, her head bob-bob-bobbing above the tops of the clover as she cried, "Ma. Ma! Ma. Ma! Want. Ma. Ma!"

She hopped across the cow pasture and

darted through a narrow gap in the barn door. Jesse and Daisy shoved aside the heavy sliding door. Emmy was standing in the middle of the barn with her head raised, having a bawling fit that shook the rafters. "Want. Ma. Ma! NOW!!!!" she repeated in an ear-piercing, heartbreaking wail.

"Can't you do something?" Daisy said, covering her ears and yelling at Jesse over the din. "Pick her up and comfort her!"

Jesse pulled the purple kneesock out of his sweatshirt pouch and put it over his hand. Then he went over and picked up the squalling baby dragon, hoping he could help.

"Hush, Emmy. Hush," he crooned to her, and snuggled her, as much as snuggling a wailing baby dragon was possible. "Jesse has you."

Whether it was the sound of his voice or the sight of the kneesock that calmed her, Emmy stopped bawling. She snorted once, blowing dragon snot everywhere, then curled against Jesse's chest. He carried her back out into the sunlight.

Just outside the barn was an area enclosed by a crumbling stone wall, where the grass grew thick and soft. Jesse and Daisy called it the Heifer Yard, and it was their favorite picnic spot. "Would

Emmy like some food?" Daisy asked in a soft but eager voice. She began to unload the backpack.

"Fooood!" cooed Emmy.

"Goooood," Daisy cooed back. She quickly peeled the hard-boiled eggs and set tiny bits of shell on the ground.

Jesse sat cross-legged and held Emmy on his lap. He reached for a piece of shell and offered it to her. She took it in her claws and sniffed it. Then she nibbled. She sighed and hiccuped and said, "Gooood."

Jesse fed her one bit of shell after another, and she crunched them up as if they were potato chips. When Jesse felt it was safe to do so, he set Emmy down gently next to her eggshell chips and let her help herself.

Then he and Daisy tucked into their soggy tuna sandwiches, with one eye on Emmy, and drank the slightly warm lemonade out of the thermos. Jesse checked his wristwatches. It was three o'clock in Goldmine City and one o'clock in the morning in Africa. He had been so excited this morning that he had not checked his e-mail. Life had gotten very busy all of a sudden.

The afternoon sun poured down on Jesse's shoulders like melted butter and made him feel drowsy. The cousins stretched out on the warm green grass as Emmy finished off the last of her chips and then curled up between them. In no time at all, the three of them were asleep.

Jesse awoke with a startled gasp and sat up. He had been dreaming that he was watching a great cloud of dust whirling down the old lane that led to the barn. At the center of the dust cloud was the million-dollar car. It took him a good few seconds of sitting there and blinking at the empty lane to convince himself that the dream wasn't real. His skin prickled with relief.

Daisy was still asleep, but Emmy was wide awake and standing on Daisy's chest, holding Daisy's gold locket in her forepaws. Emmy began cooing softly.

Daisy stirred at the sound, opened her eyes, and smiled sleepily.

"I think Emmy likes your locket," said Jesse.

"Like. Lock. Ket," the baby dragon agreed. "Like. A. Lot." Emmy held the locket and chanted, "Lock. Ket. Lock. Ket."

"That's my baby locket," Daisy said to Emmy. "It was my mother's when she was a little girl." Daisy opened the locket and showed Emmy the tiny photographs inside. Head cocked, Emmy peered at the two miniature pictures.

"See, this is my mother when she was a little girl, with her sheepdog, Fluffy. And this one here is my father holding a rock. My father always loved rocks, even when he was a little boy," Daisy said.

"Want. Lock. Ket," Emmy said, taking the locket back in her shiny green talons.

"Seems like she really, really wants it, Daze." Jesse paused thoughtfully. "Hey, do you think that's what Professor Andersson meant by hoarding . . . in his book, I mean."

Somewhat nervously, Daisy said, "Could I have my locket back please, Emmy?"

Emmy pressed it to her mouth, then held it out to Daisy.

"Lock. Ket. Back. Day. Zee."

"Thank you," said Daisy. She snapped the locket shut and tucked it back inside her T-shirt with a firm pat.

Emmy scrambled off Daisy and lit out across the Heifer Yard.

"Yikes!" yelled Daisy. "Where to now?"

Emmy disappeared into the barn. Jesse bounded to his feet and ran after her. Daisy was fast on his heels. They found Emmy perched on a long wooden shelf, examining the things in their Museum of Magic. They had been working on the collection since Jesse had arrived at Easter time, and it included anything they felt might have magical powers.

Daisy pointed to the framed pressed flowers. "Some of them heal you, some of them hurt you. Others make you strong, or brave, or smart, or calm," she explained to Emmy. "That's what it says in my herbal. That's a book Miss Alodie gave me."

"Gar. Den. Gnome," said Emmy, nodding quickly.

"Right. We never *eat* the flowers, of course," Jesse explained. "But it's fun to think about the powers they possess in their petals and stems and roots."

"Roooooots," crooned Emmy. Then she moved on to the skulls, which were Jesse's domain.

"We found these in the fields and in the Dee-Woods," he told her. "Some of them still had flesh on them and were kind of gross. So I boiled them in a pot in the Rock Shop. They're pretty clean now. The Native Americans—and some African tribes—believed that the spirits of dead animals lived on in their skulls. We've got a calf, a mouse, a dog, a wildcat, and something else we haven't figured out yet."

Emmy moved to what Jesse and Daisy called the Magical Doorknob, made of bright green crystal. "That came from the door to a magical world," Daisy explained.

Then there was the Magical Milking Stool, the Magical Potion Bottle, and the Magical Horse-shoes. "That stool is for sitting on during incantations," Jesse explained. "That blue bottle there once held potions, and those horseshoes ward off bad luck and keep you from getting struck by lightning. Then there's that stuff up there," he said, pointing to the rusty old farm tools hanging high on the barn wall. "We think that stuff might be magical, but it might just be old."

Emmy's attention was drawn to a crusty old metal ball about the size of a peach. She wrapped her arms around it and crooned.

"That," said Daisy, "is the Sorcerer's Sphere."

"See," Jesse explained to Emmy, "the man who once owned this farm wasn't just a farmer. He was a Magical Dairyman, a sorcerer. That's the sphere he used to cast his spells."

"His cows gave magical milk," said Daisy. "When you drank the milk, you had the power to fly."

"And talk to animals," Jesse said.

"And breathe underwater," Daisy added.

"At least we think so," said Jesse.

Standing on her hind legs, Emmy rolled the Sorcerer's Sphere gently back and forth. Her pulse fluttered in her throat. "Like!" she said. "Like. Lotsandlotsandlotsandlots."

"Here we go again," Daisy said. "She's definitely hoarding."

"Maybe not," said Jesse. "It's not like it's gold or anything." He stopped. *Or is it? Could there be gold beneath the dirt and the rust?*

"We found it in the brook in the pasture," Daisy told Emmy.

"We figure it belonged to the farmer. Maybe it's a piece from one of his old machines," Jesse said.

Emmy shook her head quickly. "Not," she said.

"You mean it didn't come from a machine?" Jesse asked.

"This. Old," she said. "This. Oldoldoldoldold-oldoldold."

"It's real old," Jesse said, agreeing. "The farmer moved away ages ago . . . before Daze and I were even born."

"*Old!*" Emmy insisted with a rapid shake of her head. "From. The. Time. Be. Fore!"

Jesse shot Daisy a look.

"Really?" Daisy asked. "So what is it, then?"

The dragon stood taller and looked around, as if searching the barn for the answer. Finally, she said, "I. For. Get," her eyes whirling.

"That's a big help," said Daisy.

"Show. Em. Meee," Emmy urged. "Show. Em. Meee. Where. NOW!"

"Whoa," said Jesse. "Show Emmy where now *what*?"

Emmy turned away from the Sorcerer's Sphere and launched herself off the shelf before either cousin could catch her. She lifted her arms, and the delicate web of skin beneath each arm was enough to float her to the floor like a miniature hang glider. Then she scampered out the barn door.

"Maybe she wants us to show her where we found the sphere," suggested Daisy.

When the cousins caught up with the dragon, they led her toward the brook to the spot where moss grew on the bank like tufts on a green velvet quilt.

"It was here," said Daisy, pointing at the deepest part of the brook. At this time of year, the water came up to the cousins' chests. "We found it in August, when the water was really low."

Jesse knelt down on the soft moss and dipped his hand into the water. He pulled it back. The brook, which flowed down from the Old Mother, was freezing. It wouldn't be warm enough to swim in until mid-August.

Emmy stood on the bright green moss and

stared into the silvery brook. After a while, she began to make a high humming noise, her throat throbbing wildly. She stopped, then teetered. The next thing they knew, Emmy had tumbled into the water headfirst with a SPLASH!

"Yikes!" screamed Daisy. "I can't see her. Can you?"

Jesse tried to see beneath the surface, but the reflection of the sun on the water made that nearly impossible.

Daisy was already tearing off her sneakers and socks. She pulled her sweatshirt over her head and tossed it on the bank. Then she waded into the brook and, pinching her nose between her fingers, ducked under the water.

Seconds passed and Jesse waited. What if Daisy and Emmy both drowned? Or, more likely, froze to death? He kicked off his sneakers, peeled off his socks, took a deep breath, and prepared to save them both. Just then Daisy stood up in the middle of the brook. Sputtering and coughing, she was holding Emmy high in one hand.

Daisy waded toward the bank and thrust Emmy at Jesse. "Wrap her in my sweatshirt. I have to g-g-g-go get this wet stuff off or I'm g-going to f-f-freeze to death. Plan?" Daisy didn't wait for an answer. She flapped off like a wet seal. (She and

Jesse each kept a set of clothes in the barn in an old wooden chest.)

Jesse wrapped Emmy up in Daisy's dry sweatshirt. He held her and rubbed her briskly until her shivering eased.

"Land's. Sakes!" Emmy cried, sounding just like Miss Alodie.

"What happened, Emmy?" he said.

"Fear. For. Em. Meee . . . ," she said.

"Well, I was pretty scared, too," Jesse told her.

Daisy soon came back in dry clothes, rubbing her hair with a beach towel. "What frightened you?" she asked Emmy.

"See. *Things!*" said Emmy.

"What things?" asked Daisy, plopping down on the bank.

"Bad. *Man!*" said Emmy.

"What bad man?" said Daisy. "There was no bad man down there. All I saw was rocks and moss and you . . . you poor thing."

"See. Bad. Man," Emmy said. "Bad. Man. Get. Em. Meee. Em. Meee. Sad. Help. Em. Meee. Jesse. Day. Zee. MA! MA!"

Jesse held Emmy tighter and stared at Daisy.

Daisy shrugged helplessly.

Emmy stiffened in his arms. "Saint. *George!*" she cried, then passed out.

CHAPTER SIX

LOST AND FOUND

Jesse was at the computer, the connection was working, and Professor Andersson's face was back on the screen. Daisy paced behind Jesse, holding Emmy, who had not let them put her down since she had revived from her swoon. She was still wrapped up in Daisy's sweatshirt, with a purple kneesock wound around her neck like a muffler. The little dragon was sucking away on a stalk of raw broccoli as if it were a leafy green pacifier.

Jesse clicked the mouse and said, "Can you tell us about hoarding, please?"

They heard the professor clear his throat noisily. Then his bushy white eyebrows flew up and he began to speak. "'Hoarding,' when it comes to dragons, is a misnomer."

"Who the heck is Miss Nomer?" Jesse muttered to Daisy.

Daisy reached for the dictionary, but the professor beat her to a definition. "The word means 'wrong name,'" he said. "'Hoarding' implies greed, and dragons are the least greedy of all creatures."

"Then how come he talks about hoarding in his book?" Jesse wondered aloud.

The professor continued: "In the dark years that followed The Time Before, many believed that dragons looted castle treasuries because they were greedy for riches. Now we know that this is not the case. Dragons require the properties of silver and gold and precious gems to maintain healthy bones and muscles. They quite literally absorb the minerals through their skin."

"So it's like vitamins?" Daisy asked.

"Yes, think of it as vitamins," said the professor. "Will that be all for today?"

"NO!" Jesse said. "Our baby dragon jumped into a brook," he blurted out. "She said she saw a bad man named Saint George. . . ."

"Slowly!" the professor said. "You are slurring your words. I do not understand Slurvian."

Jesse took a deep breath and repeated himself, slowly and clearly this time.

The professor furrowed his brow. "Are you absolutely certain of this?" he asked softly.

Jesse looked at Daisy. Daisy nodded. Jesse said, "Yes!"

The professor's eyes lit up, and he smiled. "My, what a precocious dragon you have! It sounds to me as if your dragon was scrying! Marvelous!"

"What's scrying?" Jesse asked.

"Dragons gaze into pools or streams and, if the circumstances—the positions of the sun in the sky and the planets in their rotations—are right, they see pictures foretelling the future. The act is called scrying. Your hatchling is very young to be scrying. She must be a very powerful dragon, but powerful or not, she still requires your protection."

"Who is Saint George?" asked Daisy.

The professor's face darkened. "Don't you know?" he said, frowning. "What are they teaching children these days?"

For a brief moment, the professor disappeared from the screen. Jesse and Daisy cried out.

Almost instantly, he appeared again and said, "Why, Saint George is the Dragon Slayer."

Daisy clutched Jesse's shoulders.

"Therefore you must protect your dragon from him at all costs," said the professor. "Remember, it is no accident that she has come to you. *She has chosen you.* Whatever you do, you must not betray that trust."

Then the computer made the irritating grinding noise and the screen went blank.

At that very moment, the back door downstairs slammed. The cousins started.

Uncle Joe called up from the kitchen, "Hey, kids! What do we feel like for dinner?"

"What's the plan?" Jesse asked Daisy.

Daisy said, "We tell him what we feel like for dinner. Then we ask him for a favor. We ask him if we can keep a pet, to be exact."

Daisy yelled down that they felt like chicken tenders and French fries. Then the cousins put their heads together to discuss the next part of their plan. It wasn't going to be easy. Uncle Joe didn't mind pets. Aunt Maggie did. It wasn't that she had anything against animals. It's just that they seemed to have had really bad luck with pets in their family.

So it was going to take some doing to convince Aunt Maggie and Uncle Joe that violating the no-pet law was a good idea. Luckily, they were starting with the easy parent.

"He's really distracted by his latest project, so *he* should be a pushover," said Daisy.

"Push. Uncle. Joe," Emmy said. "Go! Go! Joe!"

"Emmy," Daisy said sternly. "You cannot yak. You cannot say a single word. Pretend you're a very cute dumb animal. Pretend you're the cutest animal in the universe and the perfect pet for this household."

"Em. Meee. Cute," Emmy promised. "Like. Joe. Like. Lime. Stone. Like. Rock. Doc."

"Did she just make her first joke?" Jesse said, wrapping Emmy up more tightly in Daisy's sweatshirt.

"No joking. No yakking," Daisy said as she opened the door of Jesse's room. The aroma of fast food wafted up from the kitchen as they went downstairs. Uncle Joe was not much of a cook. They heard him setting the table for dinner.

"Hey, guys!" he said when he saw them. "Did you have fun gallivanting?"

"Yeah. Um, Poppy, we found something interesting in the Dell," Daisy said.

"Something really nifty," Jesse added.

Uncle Joe opened the refrigerator. Then he stopped and looked around the kitchen. "Did you guys clean today?" he asked.

Daisy winked at Jesse. "We did," she said. "After we raided the refrigerator."

"We got it back into apple-pie order," Jesse said.

Uncle Joe gave them a funny look. He took out the ketchup and the mustard and set them slowly on the table. Uncle Joe put ketchup or mustard on most things he ate. Aunt Maggie liked to say that Uncle Joe ate like an eight-year-old.

Jesse found himself checking the ceiling to make sure the relish splat hadn't reappeared. It hadn't.

"So what interesting and nifty thing did you find?" Uncle Joe asked.

Jesse uncovered Emmy's head and held out the bundle in his arms. Emmy settled her big green eyes on Uncle Joe. Uncle Joe put down the fistful of forks and knives.

"Isn't she neat?" Daisy asked.

"Wow," he said. He took a step closer. "You found her in the Dell, you say?"

The cousins nodded. They were now crossing the fingers on all four of their hands and holding their breath.

Uncle Joe took off his ROCK STAR cap and gave

his ponytail a tug. Then he put his cap back on. "No one would say that she looks like your typical barn critter," he said.

It was true. Emmy didn't look like any of the critters that lived in a barn. Emmy looked exactly like what she was. But since Uncle Joe didn't believe in dragons, he couldn't be sure what he was looking at.

"She's kind of cute for a lizard," said Uncle Joe, smiling at Emmy as Emmy again fixed her big eyes on him. "You're a little cutie," he said to her. He leaned close to her and cocked his head at the same angle as hers. "She looks like a very deep thinker, doesn't she? Makes you wonder what she'd say if she could talk."

The cousins chewed on their lips and hoped Emmy wouldn't take the cue.

"She's really tame," Daisy said.

"I think she's a green basilisk from Costa Rica," said Jesse. "Or maybe an Indian sun skink."

"Well, whatever she is, she's a long way from home," said Uncle Joe. "She must be somebody's pet that ran away. Maybe you should post some signs around town." He added, "She certainly looks valuable."

Daisy groaned. Jesse bristled. He did *not* want to put up signs all over Goldmine City. Emmy was theirs, or they were hers—either way, she didn't belong with anyone else. She had chosen the two of them. Hadn't Professor Andersson said so?

Uncle Joe looked at Daisy, then at Jesse. "Ask yourselves this, guys: How would you feel if you lost a rare pet like this and the person who found her didn't make any effort to return her to you?"

It was hard to argue with Uncle Joe about this.

"Okay, but if we put up some signs and nobody claims her after a week, can we keep her?" Daisy asked. "Can we? Can we, Poppy?"

Jesse joined in the chorus: "Can we please, Uncle Joe?"

"We named her Emmy," said Daisy.

"It's short for Emerald," Jesse said.

"Because she's green and precious," said Daisy.

Uncle Joe looked from one cousin to the other and back down at Emmy. He heaved a sigh. "Guys, this isn't exactly Fluffy, you know." He was talking about Aunt Maggie's childhood pet, the sheepdog she had loved above all other dogs. "Where would you keep her?"

Daisy smiled and winked at Jesse. Uncle Joe was showing signs of softening. "Isn't my poppy adorable?" she asked Jesse.

Jesse wasn't sure that "adorable" was the right

word for Uncle Joe, but under the circumstances he nodded vigorously.

"Where would you keep her, guys?" Uncle Joe repeated.

"For the time being," Jesse said, "she's staying in my sock drawer."

"That wouldn't cut it in the long run. She'd need a cage," said Uncle Joe.

The idea of putting Emmy in a cage made Jesse slightly ill, but he nodded along with Daisy. Then Daisy clasped her hands together and fell to her knees. "If you say you really *want* us to keep Emmy, Mom will give in. I know she will."

Uncle Joe closed his eyes. He sighed again. "I'll discuss it with her when she calls tomorrow. But no promises," he said. "I'll do my best. And you guys have to put up some FOUND signs. If nobody claims her, then we'll see. . . . *And* you have to promise you'll go online and research what kind of a lizard she is. Find out what she needs to be happy and healthy."

Jesse came close to saying, *We already have!*

After dinner, Jesse e-mailed his parents.

Dear Mom and Dad, Guess what? We have found a Costa Rican basilisk. Or maybe a sun

skink. We're putting up signs. If no one
claims her, Uncle Joe says we might get to
keep her. If Aunt Maggie says it's okay. Could
you pretty please e-mail Aunt Maggie and tell
her you think it's okay?

He heard Emmy snoring in the sock drawer
and finished his e-mail:

For now, we are keeping her in my sock
drawer. She takes after Grandma. She really
seems to have a thing for socks. Love, Jesse

Just as he was logging off, Daisy came into the
room and showed Jesse a rough layout of the sign
she had made on a page torn out of her wildflower
notebook.

"Brilliant," said Jesse.

"Thanks," said Daisy. "You take care of the
words. I'll handle the picture. Plan?"

"Plan," Jesse said. And they both set to work.

Daisy measured Emmy as best she could, from
horn to tail. "She's four inches," Daisy said to
Jesse.

Jesse nodded and added this information to the
sign he was designing on the computer.

Daisy went downstairs and came back with
Uncle Joe's digital camera. "I'm going to try very

hard to make this the worst photo I can possibly take," she announced to Jesse.

Jesse squinted at the computer screen and murmured, "You mean like those shots Uncle Joe takes of rocks?"

"Exactly right," said Daisy, peering through the camera at Emmy. "Very fuzzy and very, very, very, very boring."

By the time Daisy was ready to transfer the pictures from the camera, Jesse had the rest of the document all set to go. He had deliberately chosen a font that was hard to read. The cousins examined Daisy's photographs. They finally agreed on the most boring one to use for their sign.

"Not even Professor Andersson would be able to tell this is a baby dragon," Jesse said. He selected the picture and dropped it in at the bottom of the document. Then he saved it and printed out twelve copies of the sign:

LOST YOUR LIZARD?
FOUND.
In the area of the old dairy farm.
One green lizard,
four inches long. Greenish blue.
CONTACT DAISY AND JESSE
at 555-2245.

* * *

The next morning, Uncle Joe was already out in the Rock Shop when Jesse and Daisy brought Emmy downstairs to the kitchen. Daisy gave Emmy some lettuce leaves for breakfast. The dragon was still hungry, so Jesse fed her a whole tub of cottage cheese, then a chunk of Swiss cheese, some strawberry yogurt, a pint of coleslaw, and five small balls of mozzarella.

"She's like the Very Hungry Caterpillar!" Daisy declared.

"Hmmm," said Jesse thoughtfully, staring at Emmy's belly, which was bulging now.

Daisy lifted her up and tucked her into the hood of Jesse's sweatshirt. "She feels heavier today. Does she feel heavier to you?" Daisy asked.

"Well, of course she does. She just ate practically half the refrigerator," said Jesse, adjusting his hood.

"Poppy won't notice the missing food, but my mom will for sure when she gets back," said Daisy. "I guess we'll just have to tell her we're in training for something."

"In training to be Dragon Keepers," said Jesse with a short laugh.

Daisy put the copies of the sign in a big brown envelope and fastened it to the back of her bike with a bungee cord. Then they got on their bikes and rode into town. They stopped at every shop along Main Street and asked each shopkeeper if it was okay to put up a sign. Most of the shopkeepers were happy to let Jesse and Daisy post the signs. But when the owner of the dry cleaner's said he did not allow signs, that was okay with the cousins.

If nobody in Goldmine City ever saw a single sign, that would be fine with Jesse and Daisy. After all, Emmy had chosen them. They were the Dragon Keepers.

When they had placed the very last sign in the window of the coffee shop, Emmy, who had been watching in silence from the hood, scrambled up onto Jesse's shoulder, lifted her head, and yodeled, "Fooooood!"

"Shhhhhh!" said Daisy. "You just ate!"

"Em. Meee. Eat. More!" she said.

"Soon," said Jesse.

"Not. Soon," said Emmy. "Feed. Em. Meee. NOW!"

The cousins raced back home to boil some eggs.

"Let's boil the whole carton," said Daisy. "We can make deviled eggs for snacks, and that way we won't waste any."

As soon as the hard-boiled eggs were cool enough, they peeled them, put the shells in a bowl, and took Emmy out into the backyard. They watched her as she sat in the old sandbox and crunched her way through the eggshells.

After a while, Jesse said, "I think we need to measure her."

"I know what you mean," said Daisy. "But I'm almost afraid to." She got up, went into the house, and came back with the tape measure. She measured Emmy twice to make sure. Emmy was now eight inches long.

"Twice as long as yesterday, to be exact," said Daisy.

"Great," Jesse said gloomily.

"What if she doubles her size every day?" Daisy asked.

"She's not going to fit in the sock drawer much longer, that's for sure," Jesse said.

Daisy opened up her wildflower notebook and started writing on the back page. Jesse went to sit beside her so he could see what she was up to.

Day 1 – 4 inches
Day 2 – 8 inches
Day 3 – 16 inches
Day 4 – 32 inches

Daisy stopped writing and tossed her pencil over her shoulder. "Jeesh!" she said.

"How big do you think she's going to be when Aunt Maggie gets back?" Jesse asked worriedly.

Daisy dropped her head into her hands.

Jesse went on: "You know how she had that meltdown yesterday in the barn? That was a four-inch tantrum. . . ."

Jesse didn't need to continue, because Daisy was nodding. They were both thinking, *What would a* sixty-*four-inch meltdown look like?*

"How are we going to afford food when she gets that big? She's eating a lot now. How much is she going to need when she gets bigger? And where are we going to put her? And how are we going to keep her hidden?" Jesse was working himself into a real sweat.

Daisy lifted her head and said with a weary smile, "Take it easy, Dragon Keeper. First Kiliman-jaro, then Everest, right? Let's check in with the professor. Maybe he can help."

Daisy was just gathering up Emmy when the phone in the kitchen rang. Uncle Joe banged open the screen door of the Rock Shop and ran across the yard, up the back steps, and into the house. He caught the phone on the eighth ring. The cousins waited and crossed their fingers.

After a while, Uncle Joe kicked open the back door. He was still talking on the phone. From where the cousins were sitting, he did not look happy.

Uncle Joe crooked a finger at them.

Emmy let Jesse pop her into the pouch of his sweatshirt. As the cousins went up the steps to the back door, Jesse felt the new weight of Emmy swinging.

"No yakking," he whispered to the load in his sweatshirt.

"Em. Mee. Not. Yak," Emmy whispered back.

Uncle Joe put the phone to his chest and said to them in a low voice, "Looks like those signs of yours did the trick. This is the lizard's owner I'm talking to. He's coming over to get her."

When Uncle Joe saw the look on their faces, he held up his hand. "Easy now. You'll recall I said that I knew a lizard that rare-looking probably belonged to somebody," he said. "And this isn't just anybody. He just joined the zoology department at the College of Mining and Science. He's a well-regarded herpetologist."

"Well-regarded? A well-regarded *what*?" said Daisy. Jesse could tell that she was fighting tears.

"Herpetologist," said Uncle Joe. "A scientist who studies lizards and snakes and reptiles. I'm afraid I'll have to let him come over and get his lost lizard. I'm really very sorry, guys, but that's the way the limestone crumbles."

Uncle Joe shrugged sadly, then went back into the kitchen to give the herpetologist directions.

The cousins stared at each other in shock. Slowly, they turned around and walked back to the sandbox. Emmy had heard it all. When Jesse removed her from the pouch and set her down in the sand, she spat out a fine spray of eggshell.

"Em. Mee. Not. Go!" she growled.

"We're sorry, Emmy," said Jesse, kneeling before her. His voice was tight. "We don't have much choice."

"Em. Meee. Sad!" she keened, and keeled over into the sand.

They took her up to Jesse's room, where she curled into a tight little ball of scales. Jesse placed her gently in the sock drawer and stared at her glumly.

Daisy came to stand beside him, blinking away tears. She almost never cried, but this was a losing battle. "We need to get in touch with Professor Andersson now," she said.

"No!" said Jesse, thinking of the blazing eyes of their online advisor. "He's going to be so mad at us!"

"But don't we have to tell him?" Daisy asked.

"No. Yes. Maybe. I don't know," he said.

"Some Dragon Keepers we turned out to be," she said.

Jesse nodded, staring down at Emmy, who was once more as silent as a thunder egg. "We've only had her, what? Not even two days? It feels like my whole life! And now we're losing her."

Not long afterward, the doorbell rang, filling the house with the melody Uncle Joe had programmed it to play: "Rock of Ages."

"What if we just say no? What if we tell him, tough luck, he can't have Emmy?" Jesse said in a panic.

"I don't think Poppy would let us do that," Daisy said, wiping her nose on her sleeve. "This guy might be a giant fibber. But so are we. And we fibbed first."

"What if we hide her and say she ran away?" said Jesse.

Daisy said, "Hasn't fibbing gotten us into enough trouble already?"

"Guys!" Uncle Joe called from downstairs. "Can you bring the lizard down?"

Daisy heaved a huge sigh. "Let's get this over with."

Jesse, nodding, reached into the sock drawer and took Emmy into his hands. She felt lifeless. He didn't even need the purple kneesock, but Daisy stuffed it in her pocket anyway.

They clomped down the stairs side by side, preparing themselves to hand over their baby dragon to a complete stranger. But Jesse froze when he saw who was standing in the front hall next to Uncle Joe.

It was the man in the long black coat from High Peak. Uncle Joe had a polite smile plastered across his face. He said, "Guys, meet the man who's lost his lizard. This is Dr. St. George."

CHAPTER SEVEN

FINDERS, CHEATERS

Jesse's first thought was that Dr. St. George didn't *look* like a Dragon Slayer. He looked like a movie star. Jesse and his parents had once been bumped up to first class on a flight. A famous movie actor had been sitting across the aisle from them. Jesse couldn't stop staring at him. In the movies, the star had looked tall and handsome. Up close, he was much shorter, and his head looked huge. He was still handsome, but he was almost *too* handsome.

This man fascinated Jesse in much the same way. His big, handsome puppet head was covered with long, wavy hair the color of tarnished gold. Behind the round lenses of his wire-rim glasses, Dr. St. George's eyes were so dark and shiny, they looked varnished.

"My prize!" Dr. St. George said in a voice that was deep and low and sweet to the ear. Jesse sneaked a look at Daisy, who was staring at the stranger with her jaw hanging open.

"I'm glad the kids could help," said Uncle Joe. "What is this lizard anyway, Dr. St. George? The guys here thought she was a green basilisk from Costa Rica."

"An amateur might jump to such a conclusion," Dr. St. George said. "But she is a *Mekosuchus inexpectatus* from the island of New Caledonia. She was found in the hold of a ship that put in from the South Seas. The captain brought her to me. He didn't realize that it was the discovery of the century. You see, there hasn't been a *Mekosuchus inexpectatus* sighting since the year 1643."

St. George spoke in a voice so mesmerizing, Jesse found himself almost believing what he said, even though he knew it wasn't true.

"Gee," said Uncle Joe. "Did you hear that,

guys? This little lizard could wind up being on the evening news!"

"Dragon piddle," Jesse managed to say.

St. George brought his face close to Jesse's. Jesse recoiled. The man had shockingly bad breath.

"What did you just say?" St. George whispered.

Jesse felt a bit faint. "I said, dra—" But he winced and broke off, feeling a searing pain in his left arm where Daisy had dug her nails into his flesh.

"He wants to learn to play the *wagon fiddle*," she told St. George in a steady voice. "It's his very favorite instrument, isn't it, Jess?" She gave Jesse a most stern look, and he nodded obediently.

"Oh, yeah. Wagon fiddle," Jesse said. "It's a real old instrument. The early settlers brought them here in their, um, covered wagons."

Daisy nodded enthusiastically. "Really," she said.

"Hmmm," said Uncle Joe. "That's a new one on me."

Dr. St. George turned slowly back to Uncle Joe. "I have some tests to do to prove my theory. But I am never wrong."

"Wait a sec. What kinds of tests?" Jesse blurted out.

"Far too complex for a mere child to grasp," said

St. George, smiling at Jesse with perfect teeth.

Jesse seethed while Dr. St. George turned back to Uncle Joe and continued: "Some idiot assistant in my lab left the cage wide open two days ago. I gave him such a dressing-down. Imagine, letting my prize escape like that!" He opened a big black leather box by his feet and took out a cage with thick iron bars. It looked like the world's smallest jail cell.

"You're not going to put her in there, are you?" Jesse asked in a quavering voice.

"How would you suggest I transport her, other than in a cage?" St. George asked, looking down his nose.

Jesse glanced out the window. In front of the house was the big black million-dollar car.

Beside him, Daisy sniffled and blew her nose.

St. George reached out to take Emmy. Like lightning, Emmy uncurled from her ball and hissed at him.

"Whoa, Nelly," said Uncle Joe, taking one giant step backward.

St. George had leaped back, too. Without taking his eyes off Emmy, he pointed at Jesse and said, "You, boy, put her in the cage for me. She has grown violent in the last forty-eight hours."

"It must be the cage," said Jesse in a low growl.

But all the same, he put Emmy in the cage. It was the hardest thing he had ever had to do. Emmy seemed to understand, because she didn't lash out at him or spit at him. She only went limp and dull. Even her eyes had lost their glow.

"Good-bye, my sweet little Emmy," said Daisy with a feeble wave of her fingers. Tears rolled down her cheeks, and her nose was running.

"Sorry, Emmy," Jesse told the little dragon. He wanted to add, *Don't worry. We'll think of something.* But at the moment he had no idea what that something would or could be.

St. George was staring at both of them as if they had just burst into flame. "What did you just call it?" he whispered.

"Wh-what do you mean?" Jesse asked.

St. George's eyes pinned Jesse to the wall like a pair of darts. "You heard me. *What name did you just call it?*"

"We call her Esmeralda," he said. For some odd reason, Jesse felt it was important to keep Emmy's real name from St. George.

Daisy caught on immediately. "Yeah, after Cinderella's ugly stepsister," she added. "You know, because she's not really very beautiful. . . . Although to us, she is. . . ." Daisy's voice trailed off miserably.

Jesse held his breath. Cinderella's stepsisters

were Anastasia and Drizella, but maybe St. George wouldn't know that.

St. George's eyes narrowed, and he said, "Hmmm. Well, I have to be going now. I have tests to do."

"Wait a minute," said Daisy. She pulled up the hem of her T-shirt and wiped away her tears. Then she took the purple kneesock out of her pocket. "She needs this."

St. George stared at the sock suspiciously. "Why?"

"It's far too complex for a mere *grown-up* to grasp," Jesse said through his teeth. "She just needs it, St. George."

"That's *Dr.* St. George," he said. "And where I come from, one pronounces it *Sin* George."

"Does one?" said Jesse, dearly wishing he would go back to wherever he came from and leave them their dragon.

Daisy pushed the purple kneesock between the bars of Emmy's cage. The little dragon grasped it in her forepaws and buried her face in it.

St. George fastened the latch. He lowered the cage into the box and snapped it shut. "Good day to you all," he said, lifting the case. Then he walked out the door, his coattails flapping behind him like a cape.

Uncle Joe stared at him. Then he took off his ROCK STAR cap and tugged thoughtfully at his pony-tail. "Did you guys happen to notice that the man never even said thank you?"

The moment Jesse shut his bedroom door, Daisy exploded. "You *what*?"

Being the target of Daisy's wrath was not com-fortable. She sat down hard on Noah's bed, and he sat on Aaron's. On the carpet between them there were still bits of green and gold sparkling in the pile.

Jesse repeated what he had said to her on the way up the stairs: "I saw St. George's car parked outside our house the night before last."

"And yesterday, on the way to town . . . you saw it *again*?"

Jesse nodded, bowing his head. "Outside Miss Alodie's. And the day before, earlier, I saw him up on High Peak. I guess you and Uncle Joe were too busy to notice him. But I did. I knew he was following us. . . . Well, I did and I didn't. . . . I thought he might be, but I just wasn't sure."

"But why didn't you *say* anything to me?" she said. "If I had known, we could have come up with a plan!"

Jesse knew Daisy was right. It all seemed very

obvious to him now, but at the time . . . "I guess I didn't want to worry you if it was nothing," he said. "And all this stuff was happening . . . the thunder egg, and Emmy hatching, and getting her fed, and Professor Andersson—"

Daisy interrupted him. "We're supposed to tell each other *everything*! Isn't that what we pledged we'd do if we ever had a magical adventure? Keep the faith and tell each other *everything*? Jesse Tiger, I swear, you're worse than Edmund." Frowning, she folded her arms across her chest and looked away from him.

Jesse shook his head sadly. In *The Lion, the Witch and the Wardrobe,* Lucy's brother Edmund had been horrid, at least when he first entered into Narnia. Jesse wondered if he was really being *that* bad. Having a magical adventure was turning into a much more serious business than he had ever imagined it would be.

Daisy pounded her fists on her knees. "Oh, all *right*! I'm sorry I said you were worse than Edmund. That was mean." She sighed. "You're not horrid. And it's stupid for us to fight. We need to help Emmy, not fight about her. Let's ask Professor Andersson what to do."

Jesse bit his lip. He knew she was right.

He went over to the desk, dropped into the

chair, switched on the computer, and waited stonily for it to boot up. As soon as the professor's stern and ancient face came up on the screen, Jesse steeled himself, clicked the mouse, and began to tell him everything, starting with "There was this big black car. . . ." He spoke quickly, and he told the truth about how he had ignored the car, how they had put up the signs, how they had played right into the hands of the Dragon Slayer, and how they had lost their baby dragon.

The screen remained still and silent for such a long time that Jesse wondered if Professor Andersson had abandoned the site, leaving only his picture behind. The cousins watched his face nervously.

"Maybe you were speaking Slurvian," said Daisy. "Maybe he didn't understand you. Maybe you need to enunciate succinctly."

Jesse took a deep breath and began again. "There was this big black—"

"I HEARD YOU!" the professor thundered at them.

Jesse and Daisy shrank from the screen.

"We're really, really, really, really sorry," said Jesse in a small voice.

Professor Andersson scowled and said, "Do not waste precious time on self-recrimination."

"On *what?*" Jesse whispered to Daisy.

"Do not feel too badly," the professor explained. "No doubt you meant well. Saint George is a formidable opponent, and now at least you know what and whom you are up against."

Jesse said, "But he's a grown-up and we're just kids."

"YOU ARE DRAGON KEEPERS!" Professor Andersson roared. "Now stop sniveling and find a way to get her back. It is Saint George's intention to slay your dragon and drink her blood."

Daisy gasped.

"You have some time," the professor said. "He will not slake his thirst until she has attained a certain size."

"What size?" Jesse asked.

"I daresay you have until the end of a fortnight," he said. "A month, perhaps. It is difficult to make an accurate prediction. Each dragon grows at its own rate. And this is the first dragon born into this age—environmental influences may have some bearing."

Daisy nodded solemnly.

"Whatever that means," muttered Jesse.

"In the first four or five days of life," Professor Andersson went on, "dragons double their size every day. At that rate, by the end of two weeks she should be sufficiently sizable to—"

"Okay, okay, we get it!" Jesse said, feeling sick.

The professor's face softened. He said gently, "Your distress is not unwarranted. This could spell doom, not only for Emerald, but for the world."

"The *world*!" echoed Jesse in a hushed voice. He and Daisy exchanged looks. This was even more serious than they had thought.

Daisy placed her hand over Jesse's on the mouse and clicked. Then she leaned toward the screen and asked loudly, "How can we get her back? Can you tell us, please?"

"You are the dragon's keepers. You must find the way," Professor Andersson replied. "But know this: For as long as I can remember, Saint George has always had only one true master. And that is *greed*."

Then came the now-familiar grinding sound and the blank screen.

Jesse shook his fist. "I wish he wouldn't keep doing that," he said.

Daisy drummed her fingers on the back of Jesse's chair. "Did you happen to notice he called her Emerald?" she said thoughtfully. "He said this thing could spell doom for *Emerald*."

"I heard. That's her name, isn't it?" Jesse said

crossly, pounding the keys, trying in vain to get the site back.

"It's the name you gave her, all right. But I don't think we ever told him that," she said. "In fact, I'm one hundred percent sure we didn't."

The next morning, they ate their bowls of cereal standing over the sink. Neither tasted its crunchy goodness, but both knew they would need energy for the plan they had come up with the night before. Uncle Joe was sitting at the table with a notebook and a pile of rocks. With a sharp pencil, in tiny handwriting, he was writing a long column of numbers and letters and symbols.

The cousins rinsed out their bowls and put them in the dish drainer. Then Daisy went to stand behind her father's chair and wrapped her arms around his neck. "Poppy," she said, "we're gallivanting over to the college this morning. We want to see how Emmy's doing."

Uncle Joe looked up and stared at them with narrowed eyes. He shook his head, then went back to his notebook. "Try not to be pests," he said.

"Don't worry," said Daisy. "Dr. St. George won't even know that we're there."

When they got to the college gate, they stopped to ask where Dr. St. George's office was. The guard told them that St. George had a lab over in the basement of the Zoo. (The Zoo was what people at the college called the zoology building, where scientists and students learned about animals.)

Jesse and Daisy rode their bikes over to the Zoo and parked behind the building, near the trash cans. Then they crawled into the bushes that grew in front of the basement windows.

Daisy twitched her nose. "Do you smell that?" she whispered.

Jesse sniffed, then nodded. *Hot chili peppers!* They crawled past a set of windows looking down on long green tables crammed with cages teeming with wriggling white rats. The smell was growing stronger. They crept past a set of windows looking down on cages of monkeys. There were test tubes and beakers with chemicals, and blackboards full of numbers and symbols. The smell grew stronger still.

Finally, they came to a set of windows that were completely covered by white sheets. Unlike the other windows, these were cranked wide open, and Emmy's strong smell wafted out. Jesse lifted a corner of one sheet and looked down into the room. If he angled his head just right, he could see Emmy in her iron jail.

"I see her!" he whispered to Daisy.

Daisy peered in. "She got a lot bigger," she said.

Jesse nodded. Emmy was now the size of a large rabbit. The cage was too small for her, and the bars were pressing into her beautiful green scales. Emmy had her back to them but lifted her head at the sound of their voices. She was so cramped, she couldn't even turn around to face them.

"Jesseeee! Let. Me. Out!" she cried.

She had called out these exact words when she was inside the thunder egg. It tore Jesse's heart to hear them again. He clenched his teeth and said, "That's it. We're going in to get her now."

Daisy grabbed his leg. "Jesse, no! St. George could come back any minute! That's no plan."

Emmy called out, "Jesse! Day. Zee. Hide! Bad. Man. Come!"

Jesse let out a shaky breath and quickly lowered the sheet just enough to allow them both the tiniest peek into the laboratory. They heard the tumbling of the lock as a key turned. Beside him, Daisy stiffened and sucked in her breath. "That was a close one!" Jesse whispered.

St. George stepped into the lab. He was wearing a long white lab coat in place of the black one. He looked around the room, his wire-rims reflecting the fluorescent light and giving him that super creepy no-eyes look again. Over his nose and mouth he was holding a white handkerchief.

Daisy put her mouth up to Jesse's ear and whispered, "He hates the smell."

Jesse nodded and wondered whether being in captivity made Emmy give off an even stronger smell or if she just smelled stronger because she was bigger.

St. George leaned down and looked into Emmy's cage. He said something they couldn't hear, then took a pencil out of his lab coat pocket and poked it through the bars so that it touched Emmy's green horn.

Emmy hissed. Then she opened her mouth and spat at him.

St. George pulled back. He dropped the pencil and the handkerchief and clutched his right hand. He staggered over to a sink and ran water over the hand. The cousins, as still as statues, held their breath. Standing at the sink, St. George couldn't have been more than two feet away from them. If he had happened to look up right then, he would have seen them, as plain as the horn on Emmy's head.

St. George turned off the water and walked away. Jesse and Daisy let out their breath. He bent over and took a first-aid kit out of a cupboard. He wrapped gauze around his hand.

Daisy once more put her mouth to Jesse's ear and whispered, "Looks like she spat acid at him."

Jesse nodded. They would have to ask Professor Andersson about that.

St. George, handkerchief back over his nose and mouth, was now jotting something down on a clipboard.

Jesse tugged on Daisy's arm, and together they pulled away from the window and crawled backward out of the bushes. "I have a plan," Jesse said to Daisy.

CHAPTER EIGHT

THE DRAGON SLAYER'S DEN

Jesse shared the plan as they rode back home, pausing briefly now and then to work out the details. "Professor Andersson said Saint George was ruled by greed, right?"

"Right," said Daisy.

"Well, then, if you're greedy—greedy for dragon blood, that is—what could be better than drinking the blood of one dragon?"

Daisy thought for a second. "Drinking the blood of *two* dragons!" she said. "But, Jess, where are we going to get another dragon?"

"That's where the rest of my plan kicks in," said Jesse. He was getting excited. "What if we made a new sign? What if the sign said that a lizard a lot like Emmy had been found by some other family in Goldmine City? We won't put a phone number on the sign, just an address. It will be a real street, but it won't be a real house number."

"I get it!" said Daisy. "While he's out on the wild-goose chase, we'll rescue Emmy. But how can we be sure he'll see the sign?"

"That's the easy part. We'll hang it right under his nose. Right outside his office. He won't be able to miss it," he said. "Plan?"

"Plan," Daisy agreed.

Making a detour, they rode up into the hills to Old Mine Lane, on the far side of town, near the old boarded-up gold mine. People were always getting lost on the winding streets there. The last house on Old Mine Lane was number 499. If they put number 501 on the sign, it would completely flummox St. George.

When they got home, Jesse ran up to his room and quickly composed a new sign. He was careful to make it look nothing like the first sign. While he was busy doing this, Daisy went down to the kitchen and packed their backpack.

When they were set to go, Daisy slipped the sign into her wildflower notebook so it wouldn't wrinkle. Then Jesse and Daisy jumped on their bikes and raced back to the college. The parking lot was nearly empty except for the million-dollar car. *Everyone must be at lunch,* Jesse thought. They walked into the Zoo through the front door and tacked up the sign on a bulletin board directly across from St. George's lab. Then they got out of there fast.

Feeling very pleased with themselves, Jesse and Daisy hid in the bushes, where they had a clear view of the Zoo's front door. In silence, they munched energy bars, drank water, and waited. And waited and waited.

After a while, Daisy said, "What if he shuts the windows before he leaves?"

"I bet he won't. He can't stand the smell," said Jesse. "He needs to keep the place aired out."

"But what if he shuts them anyway?" said Daisy.

"Then we take a rock and we break a window," said Jesse.

Daisy was shocked. "Really? College property?"

Jesse nodded firmly and said, "We're Dragon Keepers. We do what we have to do."

"Right," she said, nodding along with him. "We also have to figure out where we're going to hide Emmy after we rescue her, because you know that the first place St. George is going to come looking is our house."

"Hmm," he said. "Let's not climb Everest before Kilimanjaro, okay?"

"Okay." After another long silence, Daisy said, "What time is it, Jess?"

Jesse lifted his wrist to check the time. His wrist was completely naked! He wasn't wearing either one of his wristwatches! He had no idea what time it was—here or in Africa.

Daisy grinned and punched him on the arm. "The one day you forget to wear those silly watches—"

Jesse grabbed her wrist and silenced her as the front door of the Zoo swung open. St. George stepped out, once again wearing his black coat, and looked around. Then, with their sign gripped in his hand, he strode purposefully in the direction of the parking lot.

Jesse and Daisy waited a moment, then crawled through the bushes to St. George's lab windows.

They noticed immediately that they were all closed.

"Darn it!" said Daisy.

"Hold up," said Jesse.

He pushed one of them and it swung open easily. "He must have been too excited about the other dragon to stop and lock the windows," he said.

Jesse eased himself through the window feet-first and lowered himself onto the counter next to the lab's sink. Daisy handed the backpack down to Jesse, then joined him at Emmy's cage.

"Jesse. Day. Zee. You. Came!" Emmy's green eyes sparkled.

The cousins threw their arms around the cage and did their best to hug her. "Of course we came!" Jesse said. He tried to open the cage door but, as he expected, it was locked.

"The key's got to be here somewhere," Daisy said.

"Unless he took it with him," said Jesse.

Emmy pointed her horn toward the door. Her head was the only part of her body that had any space to move. "Look!" she said.

There was a hook on the wall right next to the door, and hanging from the hook was a big ring of keys. Jesse ran to the key ring and removed it from the hook. Then he ran back to the cage and, with sweaty, fumbling fingers, began to insert one key after another into the lock.

"Hurry," said Daisy at his shoulder, flapping her hands.

"I am," said Jesse. But he had always been bad with keys.

"Let me try," said Daisy.

"I think I got it," Jesse said. The lock clicked and he pulled the cage door open. Jesse and Daisy held the cage while Emmy wiggled and squeezed herself out like a snake shedding its skin.

"Let's get out of here," said Jesse. He held out his arms for Emmy.

Emmy backed away from him. "No," she said.

"Come *on,* Emmy," said Jesse, feeling his patience tested. "I don't have a watch, and I have no idea how long St. George has been gone."

"Look!" said Emmy.

"He could come back any minute," said Daisy.

"Look!" Emmy said again.

"At what?" they both said in exasperation.

"Look. At. The. Den!" Emmy said.

The cousins took their first good look around the lab—at the den of Saint George the Dragon Slayer.

"Holy moly!" said Daisy. "I've never seen so many thunder eggs!"

There were piles and piles of thunder eggs everywhere they looked. There were thunder eggs lying in heaps near a huge, grim-looking table saw outfitted with a sharp circular blade. There was a tall trash can overflowing with thunder-egg crystals: red, blue, green, purple—every color Jesse could imagine. It was the most beautiful trash he had ever seen, all mixed up with orange rinds and paper coffee cups.

Emmy jumped down from the counter and ran across the lab, her shiny green talons clicking smartly against the tile. "Look! Look!" she said. "Here!"

Jesse and Daisy followed. Thunder eggs were simmering in pots on hot plates. The pots were labeled: "High Peak," "Popocatepetl," "Kilauea," "Fuji."

"Know what these are?" Jesse asked. "They're all volcanoes from different parts of the world."

"Look here!" said Emmy, running to the next counter, talons clicking.

They pulled open the doors of a series of squat white boxes and found more thunder eggs. These were coated with frost and labeled "Etna," "Shasta," "Krakatoa," and on and on. Who knew the world had so many volcanoes?

"This is some big-deal production he's got going on here!" said Daisy.

"Yeah, but I bet he hasn't gotten one dragon yet," Jesse said sullenly. "He had to steal ours. Can we get out of here now, please?"

"No!" said Emmy. She darted to a far corner of the room. "Look!"

With reluctance, the cousins followed her to a low table made of red leather.

"Very nice coffee table," said Jesse, arms folded. "Now can we go?"

"Look!" said Emmy. "Book!"

"I see it!" said Jesse. "But it's a *table*."

"Book!" protested Emmy.

Daisy grabbed Jesse's arm and drew him closer. "Look, Jesse Tiger," she said. "I mean, *really* look!"

He bent down and, with dawning amazement, saw what it was he was looking at. "It *is* a book!"

The cousins circled around it in wonder as Emmy looked on, pleased. It was the biggest book they had ever seen. It was bound in rich red leather, with printing stamped in gold ink, and on its front cover was a big, rusted metal ring that looked like a door knocker. The book was bigger than the ones the librarian used to read to them at story hour when they were little. It was bigger than the biggest of the ancient books Jesse had seen in museums in London and Paris and Cairo. It was a book that belonged in the library of a giant.

"Do you think it's Professor Andersson's book?" Daisy asked.

Jesse frowned. The book's cover didn't seem to have a title, only some scratchy-looking designs stamped in gold ink. If these were words, they certainly weren't in any language Jesse had ever come across. "I don't think so," he said. "It's not like this would fit on the library shelves, and Mr. Stenson would have said if it was this big . . . or written in another language . . . whatever it is."

"You're right," said Daisy, biting her lip. "Then I wonder what book it is."

"Look!" said Emmy, hopping up and down.

"I think she wants us to look inside," said Jesse.

They were standing next to the thick, gold-tooled spine, so they went around to the other side of the book and tried to open the cover. It was too heavy to lift. "You take the bottom corner," Jesse said. "I'll take the top. Ready? On the count of three: one, two, *three!*" But the cover didn't budge. Jesse stared thoughtfully at the ring. "Maybe that's some kind of a lock or something."

Just then Emmy scrabbled *clickety-click* over the top of the book and landed on the floor between them. "Some. One. Come!" she said. "Go. Now. Gonowgonowgonowgonow!!!"

They heard footsteps out in the hall. They were coming closer.

There was a knock on the door.

Jesse squeezed his eyes shut and held his breath. Dragon and kids remained rooted to the spot while the person on the other side of the door twisted the knob. Then they heard footsteps going back down the hall and, a second later, a *thunk-thunk* as the front door of the building opened and shut.

They exploded into action. Daisy unzipped the backpack, pulled out a yellow rain slicker, and thrust it at Jesse. Jesse wrapped Emmy up in it. Emmy let him pick her up without protest now. She'd gotten heavier, but he could still hold her easily.

"I'll make sure there's nobody in the hall," said Daisy. She opened the door and peered out, looking both ways. Then she took a few steps out into the hall.

"Okay!" she called back in a loud whisper. "Coast is clear!"

Jesse headed out the door, with Emmy in his arms. Before closing the door, he cast one last look over his shoulder at the giant book. *If only we could take* that *with us, too!*

Fifteen minutes later, they were back at the house and up in Jesse's bedroom.

"Let's get organized," Daisy said, her finger to her chin. "We need sleeping bags, water, food for us, food for Emmy. What else?"

Jesse and Daisy's plan was to hide with Emmy in the Deep Woods behind the barn. They had no idea how long they would have to stay there— maybe several days and nights. The Deep Woods had always seemed a little too scary for sleep-outs, but Jesse and Daisy were Dragon Keepers now, and Dragon Keepers do what they have to do. They figured that once they found a camping spot, Daisy could sneak back to the house and explain to Uncle Joe that they were camping out at the barn for a few days and ask him to pretty please not tell St. George. It was the best plan they could come up with on such short notice.

Jesse ran through the bathroom to Daisy's room and pulled their sleeping bags out of the closet while Daisy hunted around in her brothers' closet for old canteens and other camping equipment.

Emmy was crouched on the carpet by Jesse's bed, crunching her way through a head of cabbage.

From the separate rooms, the cousins called to each other.

"Don't forget the flashlight!" said Jesse.

"Right!" said Daisy.

"Make sure it has batteries!" said Jesse.

"We'll need a second backpack, don't you think?" said Daisy.

"Yeah, and what about the two-person tent—" Jesse broke off in the middle of the sentence because, just then, from Daisy's window, he saw the million-dollar car pull up to the curb.

Jesse dropped the sleeping bags and tore back through the bathroom to where Daisy was kneeling on the floor of his room, packing a second backpack. Jesse ripped it out of her hands. "Never mind about that now! He's here! St. George is here!"

CHAPTER NINE

HIDE-AND-SEEK

The doorbell rang. Jesse and Daisy grabbed each
other as the house filled with the sound of "Rock of
Ages." St. George must have been leaning on the
bell, because the tune played over and over and
over again.

Emmy rolled aside the head of cabbage and
bounded into Jesse's arms. "Bad. Man. Come!" she
whimpered. "Hidemehidemehideme!"

Over the din of the doorbell, they heard the back door slam. Uncle Joe was running through the house, calling out, "All right, all right, all right already! I'm coming!" Then they heard the front door open. Mercifully, the doorbell fell silent. A murmuring of voices came from the front hall.

Emmy had burrowed beneath Jesse's T-shirt. She was trembling. "Where can we hide her?" Jesse whispered to Daisy.

Daisy shook her head and frowned. Then her face lit up. "I know! Come with me!"

Jesse followed her down the hall to her parents' room and into Aunt Maggie's vast walk-in closet. Everything in the closet was in apple-pie order except for her shoes. Aunt Maggie had a lot of them—far too many to organize—so she kept them in three big wicker baskets in the very back of her closet.

Daisy tipped over the basket farthest from the door and dumped out all the shoes onto the floor. "Put her in there," she said to Jesse.

Jesse lifted his T-shirt. "Don't worry," he said to Emmy, "we're going to hide you really well. All you have to do is be very quiet and still." He set the dragon gently in the center of the basket. Then the cousins carefully piled shoes around and on top of her. They stood back and looked at the effect.

Emmy was completely covered, but some of the shoes were moving.

"It's fine for you to move around and get yourself comfortable," Daisy told Emmy. "But once you're settled in there, you can't move. You have to stay very, very still."

"Stay. Still. Not. Move," Emmy said from beneath the shoes. But the shoes were still moving. "Notmovenotmovenotmove." The shoes were churning around now.

Jesse sighed. "And no yakking, either," he said.

"Em. Meee. Not. Yak. Em. Meee. Eat," Emmy said. "Em. Meee. Eat. Em. Meee. Eat. *Shoe!*"

Daisy's face took on a look of pure panic. "No, Emmy! Listen to me. Do. Not. Eat. The. Shoes."

"Fooooood!" Emmy crooned.

Jesse slapped his forehead. "How can she be hungry at a time like this?"

"I'll find you something," Daisy said to Emmy. "Only please, please don't eat my mother's shoes." Daisy dashed out of the closet.

Emmy's head erupted from the pile of shoes. "Foooooooood!"

"Hush, Emmy," said Jesse sternly. "She's gone to get you something. But you *have* to keep your voice down."

Daisy flew back into the closet with a bottle of

Tums in her hand. "It says on the label that these things are loaded with calcium." She opened the bottle and dumped some of the colorful tablets into her hand. Then she knelt down and held her hand out to Emmy. "Try one and see if you like it. Quickly, please."

They watched as Emmy, with maddening slowness, took a pink tablet in her shiny green talons and nibbled at it, then popped it into her mouth and crunched it to dust. "Tums. Goooood."

"At least she won't be suffering from acid indigestion," Jesse said.

"And she can *read!*" said Daisy, tucking the open bottle next to Emmy among the shoes, then covering Emmy and the bottle with more shoes from one of the other baskets. The cousins took one last look at Emmy's basket. A soft crunching sound was coming from the pile of shoes, but at least the shoes weren't moving. They backed out and closed the closet door. Then they closed the door of the master bedroom and ran up the hall to Jesse's room.

Jesse quickly booted up the computer and slipped in the CD for a video game. Daisy rolled the head of cabbage under Jesse's bed and tidied up the evidence of their thwarted escape. Jesse was pretending to play and Daisy was pretending to watch when they heard the knock on the door they were expecting. Daisy went to answer it.

"Hi, Poppy!" said Daisy.

Her voice sounded odd. Jesse swiveled in his chair. Uncle Joe was standing in the doorway with St. George right next to him.

Seeing St. George practically inside his bedroom was enough to make Jesse want to pick up his computer and heave it at the man's big head.

"It seems," said Uncle Joe, giving them each a very careful look, "that Dr. St. George has misplaced his lizard . . . *again*."

"Gee," said Daisy, "that's too bad."

"She probably hates being in your lab," said Jesse. His hand flew to his mouth.

But St. George pounced on him. "Then you've been to my lab, have you, boy?" he said.

"Of course not!" said Daisy. "He just figured you have a lab, because you're a, whatchacallit, herpatopterist."

"Herpabologist," Jesse corrected her.

"That's *herpetologist*," said Uncle Joe. "And didn't you guys tell me you were going over to the college to visit him today?"

Daisy gave her father a scalding look.

"We decided to go to the Dell," Jesse said flatly. "We had something more important to do there."

St. George bared his perfect teeth in what passed for a smile. "I suppose you were having a *wagon fiddle* lesson instead?" He wrenched the bandaged hand out of the pocket of his coat and jabbed a finger at them. "You children aren't fooling me. You sneaked into my lab and you stole my lizard, and *I want it back!*"

Uncle Joe cleared his throat uneasily. "Um, guys, if what he's saying is true—and I'm not saying that it is—you need to come clean and tell me. The lizard isn't yours. It belongs to Dr. St. George."

Jesse said in a small voice, "But, Uncle Joe, we don't have it."

"Honest, Poppy," said Daisy.

Uncle Joe closed his eyes and sighed. "Well, fine, then. If that's the case, then you guys won't mind if we check the sock drawer? That *was* where you were keeping the lizard?"

Without waiting for an answer, Uncle Joe went to Jesse's sock drawer and opened it. He dug around in the socks for almost a minute before he said, "No lizard here." Then he turned to St. George, whose figure hung in the doorway like a long, lank, big-headed bat. "Your lizard isn't here," he said. "Sorry."

St. George said icily, "I am, too. But I'm not leaving until you've conducted a thorough search of the premises, and I mean every nook and cranny."

"Now, wait just a minute—" said Uncle Joe.

"If you refuse, I will go away and come back with the police. I promise you, we will turn your cozy little house upside down," said St. George. "My drag—er, my lizard—is here. I know it," he said, looking pointedly at Jesse, then at Daisy. "I can *smell* it."

Uncle Joe heaved a big sigh.

"Poppy, you're not going to let him—" said Daisy.

"I don't see that I have much choice," said Uncle Joe. "You know something, guys? This whole lizard thing has gotten way out of hand."

What came next felt like the world's most undelightful game of hide-and-seek as Jesse and Daisy nervously followed the two-man search party from attic to basement. By the time Uncle Joe had put his hand on the doorknob of the master bedroom, the cousins were nearly sick with anxiety.

"I thought the master bedroom was off-limits," said Jesse. (In games of hide-and-seek, they were never allowed to hide in that room.)

Uncle Joe closed his eyes and shook his head sadly. "Guys, this stopped being a game a long time ago," he said.

The cousins slouched in the doorway as St.

George looked under all the furniture and Uncle Joe went through every bureau drawer. Finally, reluctantly—and with a whispered apology to his absent wife—Uncle Joe opened the door of Aunt Maggie's closet. The closet was big enough for all of them to crowd in among Aunt Maggie's sweet-smelling racks of clothes. In such close quarters, Jesse picked up the unbearable stench of St. George's breath. Strangely, there was not a trace of the smell of hot chili peppers.

Uncle Joe took one side and St. George took the other and they worked their way down the racks. They searched every pocket and sleeve, then every drawer, every cubby, every hatbox, until at last they came to the corner where the shoes were kept.

St. George picked up the first wicker basket and dumped the shoes out onto the floor.

"Easy, buddy!" said Uncle Joe with a frown. "Some of those shoes are Italian."

St. George went through the shoes one by one. He even looked inside them, not that Emmy was small enough to fit in a shoe anymore.

Uncle Joe emptied the next basket himself, much more carefully. St. George tossed the shoes every which way. Then he seized the third basket and turned it upside down. Boots and pumps and sandals thundered to the floor, and St. George dropped to his knees and pawed through them. Any second now, Jesse expected him to find Emmy. Instead, he came up with an empty bottle of Tums and something else—something bright and sparkly.

"We *told* you we don't have your lizard," said Daisy, shooting Jesse a puzzled look. Jesse was too relieved that St. George hadn't found Emmy to worry yet about where she might have gone. "She probably ran away because you treated her so badly," Daisy said boldly. "Or maybe somebody from the Society for the Prevention of Cruelty to Lizards rescued her."

St. George held up the bright, sparkly thing in his fist. "It was here. It was! And this is my proof!" he cried. "A hoard of gold and precious gems!"

"Actually, 'hoard' is a misnomer," Jesse muttered under his breath.

"Hey," Uncle Joe said. "That happens to be the garnet necklace I gave my wife for our twenty-fifth anniversary. And I'd like it back, if you don't mind." He plucked the necklace from St. George's hand and added coldly, "We're finished here."

Dinner was a nearly silent affair. Uncle Joe had very little to say, and Jesse and Daisy kept their worries about Emmy to themselves. After they had eaten,

Uncle Joe pushed his chair away from the table and said, "I'll do the dishes. Why don't you two go upstairs and try to stay out of trouble for a while."

Jesse and Daisy nodded and went to Jesse's room. Jesse booted up the computer while Daisy watched.

"First we let him steal her and now we lose her. Professor Andersson is going to skin us alive," Jesse said.

The stern bearded face appeared on the screen, and Jesse clicked the mouse. He cleared his throat and started off with the good news: "We got Emerald back from the Dragon Slayer."

The professor's dark eyes twinkled and he stroked his beard. "Ah! Congratulations! Very good work, you two!" he said.

Jesse took a deep breath and launched into the bad news: "But then we lost her." He went on to explain, as clearly and succinctly as he could, how the Dragon Slayer had searched the house and how Emmy had disappeared from the basket of shoes where they had hidden her.

To Jesse's relief, the professor didn't even look upset. "Most intriguing!" he said. Jesse and Daisy watched his expression and waited for him to say more. At last he said, "It's possible that she has simply found herself a more effective hiding place."

"But St. George is gone," said Daisy, "and Emmy still hasn't shown up."

"Regardless of what you may have read about dragons," Professor Andersson said, "they are not aggressive. They are, by nature, prey. And so their first instinct when faced with danger is to run and hide."

"All right," Jesse said impatiently. "We already got that."

"Sometimes for years," the professor added.

Daisy draped herself over the back of Jesse's chair and groaned.

"Then again," said the professor, "there is the very slightest chance that she might be masking."

"What's that?" Jesse asked.

"Normally, dragons do not acquire the ability to mask until they are one or two years of age. But your dragon has already proved that she can scry, so she may also be an early masker."

"What is masking?" Jesse asked again.

The professor frowned in thought. "On the whole, I'd say, a very handy defense mechanism. Just as lizards such as chameleons practice camouflage, so dragons are capable of masking themselves as other creatures or things to elude predators."

In his mind, Jesse saw those insects called walking sticks, which can look like twigs. He saw tree frogs, which can look like leaves. Could Emmy be blending in with the kitchen canisters or the boxes of old records in the basement? Maybe she'd been right there among Aunt Maggie's shoes all along and they just hadn't seen her.

"Do you think she's masking somewhere in the house?" Daisy asked the professor.

The professor's response was immediate and emphatic: "NO!"

And then the screen went blank.

Jesse slammed his fists on the table. "This guy is really beginning to bug me," he said.

"At least that irritating grinding sound didn't happen this time," said Daisy. "But we still have to find Emmy on our own."

CHAPTER TEN

DRAGON IN A HAYSTACK

Uncle Joe was waiting for them when they came downstairs the next morning.

"I don't suppose you two happened to hear the phone ringing at six o'clock this morning?" Uncle Joe asked.

Daisy and Jesse looked at each other blankly and shook their heads.

"I guess we slept through it," said Daisy.

"Well, it was your buddy, St. George—"

"He is *not* our buddy," Daisy said. "We *hate* him!"

"I will grant you that he won't win any personality awards," said Uncle Joe, "but 'hate' is an awfully strong word. In any case, he wanted to know whether his lizard had shown up during the night. I don't suppose you'd tell me if it had." He eyed them both with suspicion.

"She hasn't," said Daisy.

Uncle Joe turned to Jesse with a raised eyebrow.

"No, Uncle Joe," Jesse said. "Honest! We haven't seen her!"

He gave them a last searching look. "I don't know what you guys are up to, and I don't want to know. But I think it's best if there is no gallivanting around for either of you for twenty-four hours."

Jesse's shoulders sagged. Their plan had been to search the neighborhood to see if Emmy was masking as somebody's pet or maybe even a wild bunny or a squirrel or a raccoon. How were they supposed to look for the masked Emmy if they weren't free to do a little gallivanting?

"Yes, Poppy," said Daisy sadly.

"I've got work to do," said Uncle Joe. "We made a mess yesterday searching for that lizard. I want you to go through every room in this house and put it back into apple-pie order. You two guys with the program?"

"We're with the program," Jesse and Daisy replied sulkily.

Uncle Joe stomped out the back door to the Rock Shop.

Jesse stared at the screen door. It was the first time since he had come to stay that he had seen Uncle Joe this angry. It was sort of scary.

"Don't worry," said Daisy. "After a while, he kind of forgets what he was mad about. He never stays mad."

Jesse studied Daisy's face and wondered whether she actually believed that this time.

The cousins dragged themselves through the house, room by room, putting everything back into apple-pie order. The exercise also gave them the opportunity to see whether, in spite of what the professor had said, Emmy was masking somewhere nearby. After a while, Jesse felt foolish shaking couch cushions and tapping bookends, calling out to Emmy to show herself.

Jesse had just finished straightening their bathroom and was about to make his bed when he happened to look out the window. The million-dollar car was, once again, idling at the curb. The driver's-side window was open and St. George was sitting at the wheel, watching their house.

Jesse fell to his knees and crawled through the bathroom into Daisy's room. "He's out there!" he said in a loud whisper, though he knew there was no need to keep his voice down. It wasn't as if St. George could *hear* them.

Daisy's ears turned deep pink. "Should I tell Poppy?"

"What good would that do?" said Jesse. "It's not like he's trespassing on our property or anything. He's just . . . *spying*."

"Boy," said Daisy, narrowing her eyes. "If my mom was here, she'd march right out there and tell him off but good!"

"Yeah!" said Jesse, imagining it. When Aunt Maggie told people off, they never forgot it. "Where is she when we need her?"

Daisy had gone back to fluffing pillows. Jesse joined her. "Paris, France," she said absently.

"*That's it!*" said Jesse.

"That's what?" asked Daisy.

"That's where she is!" said Jesse.

Daisy stopped fluffing and gave him a weird look. "Emmy's in Paris, France?"

"No! Remember the other day when Emmy was in the Dell and she was crying for her mama and everything? For some reason, she seems to think her mother is there. And that's where she is. She isn't masking! She's gone to find her mother, like everybody does when they're scared!"

Daisy's face brightened up by a few watts. "You think?"

"I *know,* Daze! Let's go!" He ran to the door and stopped. "Oh, right. We can't go. We're grounded. And even if we could go, it's probably not such a hot idea anyway, if *you-know-who* is spying on us out front. What if he followed us?" Jesse shuddered at the thought of St. George invading the Dell.

Daisy tucked her hair behind her ears, completely unfazed. "He can't see us in the backyard if he's sitting out front. It's perfectly safe to go back to the Dell. And Poppy wouldn't even count it as gallivanting. The Dell is practically our second home!"

Daisy snagged another bottle of Tums off the kitchen shelf on their way out. "Just in case she's hungry," she explained with a wide grin.

"Or has acid indigestion," said Jesse, grinning back. Now that they were back on track, their spirits were rising.

They slipped out the back, careful not to let the screen door slam behind them. They went down the steps, dropped to all fours, and started crawling across the backyard on their elbows, commando-style.

The Dell might be home turf as far as they were concerned, but they did not want to test their opinion in the court of Uncle Joe.

They crawled past the Rock Shop's window. Then they got up and ran in a crouching position, dodging from shrub to shrub, until they had made it to the top of the rise and the laurel patch. There they dived into the bushes and crawled through them at double time. Just when their knees started giving out, they came to the end of the tunnel and stood up.

Jesse and Daisy scanned the Dell. But there was no sign of Emmy.

"She's in the barn," said Jesse with a good deal more confidence than he felt.

They ran down the hill toward the barn, cut across the Heifer Yard, and threw themselves against the barn's heavy sliding door. Then they dragged it open. Jesse blinked the sunlight out of his eyes and peered into the shadows of the barn. There was no sign of Emmy here, either, but Jesse noticed something right away: the Sorcerer's Sphere was missing!

Daisy noticed, too, because she turned to Jesse and asked, "Did you hide it somewhere?"

Jesse shook his head. "She must have it."

"What makes you so sure?" Daisy asked.

Jesse lifted up his face and sniffed. He cocked his thumb toward the ceiling. "She's up there," he said, "in the hayloft."

The ladder to the hayloft was in a far corner of the barn. It was spattered with pigeon poop and one of its rungs was a little loose and creaky, but Jesse and Daisy clambered up. The higher they climbed, the stronger the smell of hot chili peppers. The ladder rose through a square hole in the hayloft floor. Jesse entered the hayloft first, followed quickly by Daisy.

Emmy was sitting on the Magical Milking Stool in the center of the loft. Since they had last seen her, she had grown to the size of an adult chimpanzee. She was holding the Sorcerer's Sphere between her shiny green talons.

"Jesse and Daisy!"

"Emmy!" They ran to her and threw their arms around her. There was more than enough of her now for both of them to hug at the same time. Emmy tilted her head from side to side and nuzzled each of them.

Suddenly they heard the sound of a car motor revving, growing louder by the second. Jesse ran to a wall and peered through a wide chink in the barn siding.

In a great cloud of dust, the big black million-dollar car was coming down the lane. This was exactly like the dream Jesse had had when he fell asleep in the Heifer Yard!

"It's him!" Jesse said. "He's coming!"

"The Deep Woods!" said Daisy. "Let's make a run for it!"

Jesse's face felt glued to the chink in the barn wall. "We'll never make it," he said.

"Bad man come!" Emmy whimpered.

"She sounds a lot less like a baby now, don't you think, Jess?" Daisy said.

Jesse turned back to Daisy. There was no time to think about what Emmy sounded like. "We need to do something, Daze!" he said, his voice rising in panic.

"We can't just stand here and let him find her," said Daisy, her hands flapping. "We have to hide her!"

But where? The two of them looked around the hayloft. In all their years of playing hide-and-seek, they had never bothered much with the hayloft. Hiding there would be like hiding in a football field. Then Jesse's eyes fell upon the solution.

The farmer had left behind some bales of hay. The hay had been sitting up in the dry heat of the hayloft for so long that it had practically turned to dust, but it would have to do.

Daisy was already by the hay, hands on hips, checking out the bales. "What do you think?" she said.

"It's our only choice," said Jesse.

Just outside, they heard the squeal of brakes, then the slamming of car doors.

"Emmy, give me the sphere," Jesse said. Reluctantly, Emmy handed it to him. Jesse forced it into his back pocket. "Emmy, follow me," he said. He led her over to the bales. The string holding the bales together was so old, it broke easily. "Emmy, stand here. Stand very still. We're going to be throwing hay on top of you, and you just have to let us. It's the only way to hide you from the bad man."

Jesse and Daisy dug in and started throwing armloads of loose hay on top of Emmy. Emmy sputtered. "Not like! Itchy!"

"Sorry, Emmy!" Jesse said. "It's the only way!"

"Emmy hide self," she said. She curled up so that she became a glittering green beach ball with two dark stripes.

"Do you think she's masking?" Jesse asked as they continued to bury her in hay.

"I think she's just curling up into a ball because she's terrified," said Daisy. "Can you blame her?"

They heard voices from below: St. George's, low and sweet, and someone else's. It was Uncle Joe's! It sounded as if they were arguing.

Jesse and Daisy sped up the hay-flinging. By now, Emmy was completely buried in a mound of hay that rose up higher than the cousins' heads. At last, Jesse and Daisy stopped heaving hay. They looked at each other and nodded, panting and covered in hay dust. This would have to do. They dusted each other off quickly. Then Jesse and Daisy settled themselves into the side of the mountain of hay and waited.

Jesse slowed his breathing down and tried to look calm and comfortable, but his heart was hammering and little bits of straw were poking him through his clothing. Emmy was right: the hay *was* itchy. The Sorcerer's Sphere felt like the world's biggest boil on his bottom.

Daisy grabbed his hand as they heard the loose rung creak beneath someone's weight. Under them, beneath the hay, Jesse felt Emmy breathing in and out, in and out, very fast.

Uncle Joe popped up through the hole in the hayloft floor. "Hey there!" he called, then chuckled. "Pun intended," he added. He climbed into the loft.

"You guys are gallivanting around when I told you not to," he said, waggling his finger at them. "But I had a hunch you'd count the barn as home turf, and I was right! I'm afraid I've brought you a little company. Your favorite herpetopterist is here," he finished with a wink.

Then St. George's big head poked up through the hole and the rest of him followed, black as a hearse in a dust storm. His eyeglasses flashed in the loft's semidarkness as he paced about, the tails of his coat trailing across the wooden planks. He stopped suddenly and whirled upon them.

"You *thieves*!" he said.

Jesse felt Daisy tense up beside him, but Jesse was tired of St. George's accusations. "We are not! She's not your lizard," he said. "And we're sick of hearing you say that. She's ours, and you're the one who stole her from us."

"Really?" said Uncle Joe, sounding somewhat surprised.

"Really!" said Daisy.

"Then you *do* have her!" said St. George. "Of course you do! You've had her all along!"

Uncle Joe's eyebrows went up.

"We do *not*," said Daisy quickly.

"She's not here," Jesse said, feeling bolder by

the second. "She's not here because you scared her away. You scared her away because you're a bad, *bad* man."

Without taking his eyes off the cousins, St. George said to Uncle Joe, "Your children are rather adept storytellers." His eyes, behind the round disks of his glasses, looked empty.

Uncle Joe looked from Daisy and Jesse to St. George. He didn't know who to believe.

"I have an idea," said St. George with a bland smile. "Let's produce the lizard, and then we'll resolve the issue of its ownership."

"That sounds fair to me," said Uncle Joe.

"Poppy!" Daisy protested.

St. George stalked around the loft, peering into the dark corners. Then he backed up and stumbled over the Magic Milking Stool. "Get this thing out of my way!" he growled. He picked it up and flung it carelessly aside. Jesse watched the milking stool go sailing high into the air and marveled at St. George's strength as the stool crashed clean through the side of the barn and out into the Heifer Yard.

"Hey! Watch it!" said Uncle Joe. "This is a beautiful old barn, and it's not your property!"

St. George turned back to face him. "Nor is it

yours, sir. And letting these mischievous brats use it as their playhouse is reprehensible, irresponsible, *and*, I might add, illegal."

"There's no call to get nasty," said Uncle Joe. "Let's just find the lizard, shall we, and get on with our day."

Daisy shook her head. Jesse sighed. He knew that his uncle meant well, but he wasn't being much of a help.

"She is here!" St. George shouted. "I know this because I can smell her! I would know that disgusting stink anywhere!"

"She does not stink!" Daisy said indignantly. Jesse gave her a swift, sharp elbow to the ribs.

"You should talk," Jesse said boldly. *Dr. Dead-Rat Breath,* he added silently.

St. George glared at Jesse as if he had heard his thoughts. "Get up," he told them.

Daisy looked to her father. "Do we have to do what he says, Poppy?"

"Can we please just get this over with?" said Uncle Joe.

The cousins sighed and looked at each other. They unlocked their hands, slowly got up, and stepped away from the makeshift haystack.

"Would you please assist me?" St. George asked Uncle Joe.

"You know something, buddy?" said Uncle Joe, folding his arms across his chest. "You want to dig around in that dusty old hay, you can do it yourself."

Daisy and Jesse went to stand next to Uncle Joe. Uncle Joe put an arm around each cousin and drew them close. Daisy hid her face in her father's chest. Jesse clenched his fists and watched as St. George dug into the hay, picked it up by the armful, and heaved it aside.

Each time St. George dug into the hay, Jesse flinched. It was just a matter of time before he found Emmy. It was just a matter of time before it was all over for all of them. He remembered Professor Andersson's words—*doom*, for both Emmy and the world—and shivered.

Suddenly the entire stack started shifting from side to side, as if it had come alive. Hay began to fly every which way. St. George staggered backward. The air was full of flying straw and the smell of red-hot chili peppers.

Bit by bit, the hay storm settled.

There, standing in the middle of the fallen hay, was a large and very shaggy white sheepdog. Her long pink tongue lolled out of her mouth. Her stubby white tail thumped on the floor of the hayloft. She jumped on top of St. George and knocked him backward, onto the floor. She started licking him so hard, she knocked the glasses off his face.

Jesse hoped no one—except Daisy—would notice that her long pink tongue was forked.

"Fluffy?" Uncle Joe shouted, as if he couldn't believe his eyes, either—but for different reasons altogether.

"Get it off me," St. George whined. "I hate dogs!"

"'Hate' is such a strong word," said Jesse, trying very hard not to smile.

CHAPTER ELEVEN

OUTDOOR DOG

Two days later, Aunt Maggie came back from Paris. She stepped out of the cab and started for the door, then stopped short on the walk. Jesse and Daisy and Emmy were gathered on the front step, waiting for her. Emmy was in her sheepdog disguise, and Jesse and Daisy held their breath as Aunt Maggie stared. Then Aunt Maggie dropped her bags and ran up the walk toward them. She threw her arms around the dog, burying her face in its thick snow-white fur.

Jesse caught Daisy's eye. It was still hard for them to believe that Emmy could mask herself so completely that she even *felt* like a sheepdog.

"She's adorable!" Aunt Maggie said. "Where did you get her?"

"From Miss Alodie," the cousins replied in unison.

Then Jesse and Daisy went on to tell her the same fib they had told Uncle Joe in the hayloft the other day. It was as if the lie had settled and taken root in both their brains at the same time. It was Miss Alodie, they said. Miss Alodie had given them the sheepdog. Wasn't that sweet of Miss Alodie?

After all the odd things that had happened in the last week, Uncle Joe wasn't sure he believed them. So Uncle Joe had called up Miss Alodie right away. And the funny thing was, the same fib seemed to have found its way into Miss Alodie's brain. Only bigger and better.

Miss Alodie said that her niece was leaving the farm where she had lived all her life to go away to college. Of course, no dogs were allowed at the niece's college. The niece had left the dog with

Aunt Alodie, but she was afraid that it would dig up her beautiful flower beds. So she was very happy when Daisy and Jesse came along and offered to take the dog off her hands.

"And she'll stay in the garage," said Jesse, winking at Daisy, "so the house can stay in apple-pie order."

"Oh, she doesn't have to stay in the garage," said Aunt Maggie. "She's welcome to stay in the house."

"Oh, no!" said Daisy. "She really likes the garage!"

Emmy did like the garage. "Very nice cave," she had told them.

"On the farm, she stayed outside," Jesse explained to Aunt Maggie. "She's what they call an outdoor dog. You know, like Lassie. She gets nervous inside. And we wouldn't want any accidents to happen in there."

Aunt Maggie hugged Emmy and said, "Okay, then. Why not? We've certainly never used it for cars. And what is this around her neck?"

"Those are my purple kneesocks tied together to make a collar," Daisy told her. "She really likes my socks."

"This dog needs a proper collar," said Aunt

Maggie. "And a leash, too. You'll need to walk her. And keep her tied up when you're not around. If she ran away or got hit by a car—" She bit her lip and shut her eyes.

Jesse looked at Daisy with raised eyebrows. He wasn't sure how well a collar and a leash and being tied up were going to go over with Emmy.

"Having a pet like this is a great responsibility, you know," said Aunt Maggie.

"We know," Jesse and Daisy chimed.

"One more thing, Mom," Daisy said. "Remember how you said that one day I could give my baby locket away to someone I really loved?"

"I remember," Aunt Maggie said, looking worried.

"Well," said Daisy, "I've found somebody I want to give it away to."

After a long pause, Aunt Maggie said, "Daisy, honey, is this some boy you've met? Because if it's a boy, I think you are way too young—"

"It's not a boy, Mom. It's a girl. It's Emmy. I want to give my baby locket to Emmy. I love Emmy more than anything in the world, and I want her to have it forever and ever."

Aunt Maggie gasped. "Oh, Daisy, how did you know?"

"How did I know what, Mom?"

"That I put that baby locket on my own Fluffy's collar when I was a little girl, too."

That night, Jesse e-mailed his parents:

Dear Mom and Dad, Daisy and I have a new pet. Guess what? She's a sheepdog. Just like Aunt Maggie's old dog Fluffy. Her name is Emmy. Short for Emerald. Don't ask why—it would take too long to explain. She's a great dog. She is so great, I might have to stay here longer than a year. Can we talk? I have a plan. Love, your son, Jesse

KATE KLIMO first got the idea for this book many years ago when her three sons were small and she came across a geode lying among the rolled-up socks in one of their sock drawers. Now that her sons are all grown up, she has finally found the time to write the story down. When she is not writing, Kate is a children's book publisher. She lives in upstate New York with her husband, Harry, three horses, and one grandcat.